FISH Finelli

BOOK 3

Text copyright © 2015 by E. S. Farber.
Illustrations copyright © 2015 by Jessica Warrick.

Library of Congress Cataloging-in-Publication Data:

Farber, Erica, author.
Ghosts don't wear glasses / by E. S. Farber; illustrated by Jessica Warrick.
pages cm. — (Fish Finelli ; book 3)
Summary: In order to fulfill a bet with Bryce, his nemesis, Fish has to go into the Hannibal
W. Royce house, which is said to be haunted by the ghost of a whaling captain, and bring out
the whaler's harpoon, which is supposedly dripping with blood.
ISBN 978-1-4521-3815-2
1. Haunted houses—Juvenile fiction. 2. Whalers (Persons)—Juvenile fiction. 3. Ghost
stories. 4. Bullying—Juvenile fiction. 5. Wagers—Juvenile fiction. 6. Friendship—Juvenile
fiction. [1. Haunted houses—Fiction. 2. Whalers (Persons)—Fiction. 3. Ghosts—Fiction. 4.
Bullying—Fiction. 5. Wagers—Fiction. 6. Friendship—Fiction.] I. Warrick, Jessica, illustrator.
II. Title. III. Title: Ghosts do not wear glasses.
PZ7.F22275Gj 2015
813.6—dc23
[Fic]
2014047356

Manufactured in China.

MIX
Paper from
responsible sources
FSC www.fsc.org FSC™ C101537

Design by Tara Creehan.
Typeset in Century Schoolbook.

10 9 8 7 6 5 4 3 2 1

Chronicle Books LLC
680 Second Street
San Francisco, CA 94107

Chronicle Books—we see things differently.
Become part of our community at www.chroniclekids.com.

GHOSTS DON'T WEAR GLASSES

BY E. S. FARBER • ILLUSTRATED BY JESSICA WARRICK

chronicle books · san francisco

A DATE WITH DOOM

"Once, twice, three—shoot!"

Roger and T. J. flung out their hands. Roger's was in a fist. T. J.'s was flat.

"Paper covers rock!" said T. J. "I win!"

"You went a split second after me," said Roger. "Do over."

"That's what you said the last three times," said T. J.

It was a hot Wednesday afternoon. We were on our way to the Whooping Hollow One Stop with a wagon full of cans and bottles to recycle. Once we cashed them in, we were going to use the money for ice cream at Toot Sweets.

"He's right, Roger," I said. "It's your turn to pull. And quit talking. I'm trying to calculate the volume of the wagon, which is a rectangular prism, and multiply it by point-oh-five to figure out how much money we're going to get."

"Fish, it's vacation, which means no more decimals. Hooray! One more time, Teej, pretty please with chocolate-chip pancakes and cheese fries on top," said Roger.

T. J. shrugged.

"And now for the Spanish version," said Roger. "*Uno, dos, tres*—shoot!"

"Rock smashes scissors!" said T. J. "I win—again."

Roger sighed dramatically as he grabbed the wagon handle.

"What are you going to get?" said T. J. "I'm thinking two scoops of bubble-gum ice cream with sour gummies."

"Ew, T. J.! Bubble gum is nasty with sours," said Roger. "Blueberry Bomb or Pineapple Pizazz are much better."

"Reality check, guys," I said. "There's not going to be enough money for double scoops with toppings for each of us. Those cost four dollars and fifty cents, which means we need thirteen dollars and fifty cents plus tax. If the volume of the wagon is roughly one hundred and seventy-two cubic inches, that's not—"

"Dude, we've got hundreds of bottles and cans here," said Roger as we crossed the railroad tracks onto Main Street. "Fourteen, fifteen bucks, I bet. Your turn." He thrust the wagon handle into my hand and raced ahead before I could open my mouth.

T. J. and I caught up with Roger about a block from Toot Sweets. The line was already out the door.

"Boo!" Micah and Silas King popped out from behind the mailbox between Get Whooped, the surfer shop, and Toot Sweets. They're twins a year older than we are who run a clam stand on Two Mile Harbor.

"Hey, dudes," said Roger, as we all bumped fists. "Clam business slow? Need us to help you out and find some oysters?"

We had briefly worked for the twins earlier in the summer so we could pay their older brother, Eli, to help us fix up our boat, the *Fireball,* to get it ready to race in the Captain Kidd Classic.

"My offer still stands," said Mi, flipping through a fat wad of dollar bills and counting them under his breath. "You get fifty percent of whatever you catch—oysters or clams."

"And I still say seventy-five percent is only fair," said Roger.

"It's a better get-rich-quick scheme than *that,*" said Mi, tilting his head toward the wagon.

"This isn't a get-rich-quick scheme," said Roger. "We're recycling, helping to save the planet and the polar bears so their ice caps don't sink."

"You mean melt," I said. "Due to global warming caused partly by the erosion of the ozone layer as a result of our use of fossil fuels and the carbon—"

"It's summer vacation, Great Brain, please," said Roger.

"Tell me you're not in it for the money," said Mi.

I laughed. "He got you, Rog, since you're not getting a double scoop with toppings without it."

"Are you guys really going into the one-legged whaler's haunted house?" asked Si all of a sudden, pushing his glasses back up on his nose. "Even with the doorway crying blood and everything?"

"What?" I said, my heart beating faster in my chest.

I had been trying to forget about my dare with Bryce Billings, the bully of Whooping Hollow Elementary who thinks he is the coolest dude ever. We're supposed to go into that house and bring out the whaler's bloody harpoon.

That's right, his bloody harpoon. It's a long story, and believe it or not, I made up the dare myself. When I lose my temper, I say stuff that surprises even me.

"Burt Babinski said he saw the blood himself, dripping right down the front door," said Si.

"Hey," said T. J., pointing to the *Whooping Hollow Star* newspapers in the kiosk next to the mailbox. "Look!"

Roger read the headline aloud: "WHOOPING HOLLOW WHALER'S HOUSE FOR SALE."

"The Hannibal W. Royce house, built in 1845 by the famous one-legged whaling captain and Whooping Hollow legend, is soon to be for sale," I read.

"No wonder the house is crying blood," said T. J.

"It's not like it's true," I said. "Doors can't bleed."

"Fish has a point there, Teej," said Roger. "I mean, we're talking Burt Babinski. The same individual who claimed that he had been struck by lightning while taking a shower, which is how come he now has X-ray vision."

"So, when you going in?" asked Mi, looking up from his wad of cash.

"I don't know," I said. "We have to set the date with Bryce."

"A date with doom," said Si solemnly.

"I wouldn't want to be in your shoes," said Mi.

"Is that because you're more of a flip-flop sort of guy?" joked Roger.

"You know what I mean," said Mi. "Not that I believe in ghosts, but if I were a ghost, the one-legged whaler's house is just the kind of creepy place I'd call home."

"The legend is that the whaler's ghost stabs anyone through the heart with his bloody harpoon who dares to enter that house," said Si, blinking behind his glasses. "'Cause a killer white whale bit his leg off and he's still mad about it all these hundreds of years later."

"You mean a *right* whale, not a white whale," I said. "Whalers hunted right whales because they had the most blubber. That's why they were called right whales.

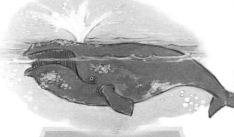

Right Whales

About 50 feet long, weighing up to 70 tons (140,000 thousand pounds), they have hairy heads with bumpy patches of skin, small eyes, and two blowholes. Named right whales by whalers because they were the "right" whales to hunt since they were slow swimmers (averaging 6 miles per hour), making them easy to catch, and had thick blubber that could be turned into lots of oil. So few are left, they are endangered.

And they weren't killers. The orca, though it's known as the killer whale—"

"Enough with the marine science, O, Great Brainio," said Roger.

"I hope Bryce forgets about the dare," said Si. "For your sake."

"Not likely," said Mi. "Since I heard his dad is the one who is trying to buy the house in the first place."

"Like I said, that explains the bleeding," said T. J., his brow furrowed. "Dr. Ghost B. Gone says that sometimes when an entity gets upset, it acts out in ways the living can see. So I bet the entity is upset that the house is being sold."

"Entity?" asked Si.

"That's what Dr. Ghost B. Gone calls ghosts," said T. J. "It's the technical name."

Dr. Ghost B. Gone is T. J.'s favorite TV show. It's about a crazy ghost hunter who investigates hauntings. T. J.'s also not allowed to watch it, because it's on at ten o'clock at night and it's creepy. So he sneaks behind his dad's recliner while his parents watch the show.

"It takes a really powerful entity to make a door drip blood," T. J. said. "That means this ghost is not an orb or poltergeist or streak. I'm afraid to say it sounds like the work of an elemental."

"What in the heck is an elemental?" I asked. Not that I believe in ghosts or anything.

"It's *all* mental, if you ask me," said Roger, twirling his index finger around his right ear.

"No, it's not," said T. J. in the serious voice he uses with teachers and his mom. "There's lots of proof ghosts exist. An elemental is an entity that can take full physical form. Dr. Ghost B. Gone says you have to be very careful when you deal with one because an elemental can—"

"It's elementary, my dear Watson," Roger said in a fake English accent.

"An elemental can what?" asked Si, his green eyes bulging like a frog's behind his glasses.

Before T. J. could answer, the line began to move and a group of kids came out of Toot Sweets. One of them had slicked-back blond hair and was wearing a Sandstone Country Club rash guard, board shorts, and the gold-rimmed sunglasses I knew only too well. Bryce had gotten them after our first bet. He lost that bet and had to give me his mirrored sunglasses when we found Captain Kidd's treasure.

I could see his trusty sidekick, Trippy, and his new best buddy, True, a boy I didn't know because he belonged to the club and only lived here in the summer.

"Incoming!" said Roger.

I looked away, hoping Bryce wouldn't see me.

"Oooh, check out the trash collectors," said Bryce with a smirk on his face. Behind him, Trippy and True snickered. "Hey, I think I have something for you."

Bryce handed Trippy his chocolate ice cream cone and pulled something out of his backpack. It was a not-quite-empty Gatorade bottle. Before I could make a move, he tossed it into the wagon. Blue Gatorade dripped all over the cans.

"Hey!" I said, my face burning. "Take that back."

"Why?" said Bryce. "It's garbage and you're collecting garbage, right?"

Heads turned. Bryce had that effect on people. If we were amphibians in a tropical rain forest, he'd be the bright-yellow poison dart frog, deadly and impossible to miss. I'd be a panther chameleon, changing colors to blend into the background—except for when I lose my temper and open my big mouth, that is.

"Not yours," I said, feeling my ears start burning, too, as I grabbed the Gatorade bottle. I wanted to throw it at him, but I just tossed it onto the ground by his feet.

"Sorry," said Bryce without sounding sorry at all. "I thought you could use the five cents." Trippy and True snickered again.

"How dare you?" I began, my hands balling into fists.

"Speaking of dares, Mr. 'I'm so brave I'll go into the one-legged whaler's haunted house and bring out his bloody harpoon,'" said Bryce in a high-pitched voice, as if he were imitating a girl, "when are you planning to go into the house?"

More eyes turned our way.

"Any day now," I said as Roger and T. J. glanced over at me in surprise.

SNORT. "It better be, because my dad is going to bulldoze that place soon. Unless you're too chicken . . ."

"Bawk! Bawk!" said Trippy, flapping his arms.

"Bawk! Bawk!" said True, flapping, too.

"I'm not chicken," I said, my face turning an even deeper shade of red.

"You know what they say about that house?" said Bryce, dropping his voice to a loud whisper. "People go in and never

come out. The whaler's ghost stabs them with his bloody harpoon right through the heart and then he puts their bodies in the basement, which is filled with the bones from all the dead people he already stabbed. Remember what happened to that paperboy who didn't know the house was haunted?"

A murmur ran through the crowd.

"He went to deliver the paper and then he was never heard from again. All they found was his bloody baseball cap. He's down there, too, in that basement, his body slowly turning into a rotting corpse."

T. J. and Roger stiffened beside me.

"That's just a story," I said, although it sure was creepy.

Just then a girl with long black hair pushed her way toward Bryce. She was wearing a wetsuit and holding a vanilla ice cream cone.

"Ready to go?" she said.

"Hi, Clementine!" My face got hot again. I bet I was as red as my mom's cherry Jell-O.

"Hi, Fish!" She smiled, happy to see me.

Clementine had won the Captain Kidd Classic boat race. Besides being an excellent mariner, she also happens to be just about the prettiest girl in the world. She hangs out with

Bryce because his parents are friends with her dad and they live next door to each other. Even though he's nasty to me and so many other kids, he's always real nice to her.

"You mean 'Hi, chicken,'" said Bryce.

"I'm not chicken!"

"Bawk! Bawk!" All three boys flapped their arms.

A couple of kids laughed.

"Yeah," said Roger. "He's not chicken. He's going into the one-legged whaler's haunted house, just like he said."

"My father says out with the old, in with the new. He's going to put up a bunch of luxury condos with a private golf course and a spa." Bryce's father wasn't known as the real estate king for nothing. "Who cares about some old whaler, anyway? He's dead. He killed some whales. Big deal."

"I sure hope you don't get stabbed by the bloody harpoon, Finelli," called our friend Two O from farther up the line.

"Just admit it, loser," said Bryce. "You're afraid of the ghost, which is why you haven't gone in there. And so are your little chicken friends."

"Quit calling me a loser." All eyes were on me, including Clementine's. "I'm not scared and neither are my friends."

"Yeah," said Roger.

T. J. was madly chewing his gum, his face pale. Roger elbowed him.

"Um . . . yeah . . ."

"We've just been waiting for . . ." What, I wondered. Special equipment? Information? The right moment? That was it! The right moment. How had I forgotten? Although it looked like Bryce had forgotten, too.

"Guts? Since you obviously don't have any," said Bryce, high-fiving Trippy.

"We've got plenty of guts," I said, gritting my teeth. "We've just been waiting for the full moon, like you dared me, remember? It was your idea."

"Yup," said Roger.

"So, the night of the full moon is when we're going in."

"Right," sneered Bryce. "You're all talk, chicken!"

"I am NOT." How dare Bryce call me a liar? I was about to boil over, like molten lava out of a volcano.

"I think Saturday night is a full moon," said Clementine. "I bet that's when Fish was planning to go into the whaler's house. Weren't you, Fish?"

I nodded. Saturday night was the night of the full moon. Uncle Norman had asked my dad to go midnight fishing for stripers then. He always says the full moon is the best time to catch them.

"So, Saturday night it is. We'll meet you at the one-legged whaler's at eight o'clock." I glared at Bryce.

"Just before moonrise," said Roger.

"Be there, or everyone will know the truth," said Bryce, taking a bite of his cone. He stalked off before I could say another word.

"BAWK! BAWK!" Trippy and True flapped their arms, laughing as they headed after him.

Clementine gave me a thumbs-up before she followed.

"Good luck on your date with doom!" said Mi.

"You're going to need it . . . ," added Si.

SEE YOU TombMORROW!

"It's my turn," said Roger.

"It's still my turn," said T. J.

"Come on, Teej," said Roger. "I can't help it if my machine is out of service." He kicked it once.

I kept feeding cans into my machine, listening to the satisfying clink of nickels, dimes, and quarters collecting in the change return.

"I know. Let's shoot for it," said Roger.

"Enough with the shooting, Rog," I said.

"Let me use your machine, then," said Roger.

I was about to tell him to start counting the change when a voice behind us said, "Excuse me. Can you tell me how to get to Raven Hill Road?"

The three of us whipped around. There was only one place on Raven Hill Road anyone ever went.

"Are you going to the one-legged whaler's house?" asked T. J.

"Is that what they call it?" asked the guy, who had one of those big hiking backpacks with a frame. I noticed he didn't answer the question.

"You know, it's haunted," T. J. went on.

The guy shifted the backpack all of a sudden, looking uncomfortable. He was in his early twenties, dressed in jeans and hiking boots. He wore a T-shirt with a picture of a shovel on it that said: *Archaeologists Dig It!* I smiled. No wonder the guy was uncomfortable. He was an archaeologist—you know, someone who digs up old pieces of pottery and metal and stones and stuff. Archaeologists study history. They believe in facts, not ghosts.

"He's ghost crazy," I said. "Don't listen to him."

"When you face an unknown entity," T. J. began reciting, "Dr. Ghost B. Gone always says to walk softly and carry a big flashlight."

The guy started coughing like his spit went down his trachea instead of his esophagus. He looked real startled.

"It's not far," I said, to get the conversation away from ghosts, since, like I said, archaeologists like facts.

"You hang a left out of the parking lot," said Roger. "That will put you on forty-four, Harbor Road. You take that past two stop signs."

"No, three," I said.

The guy opened his backpack and pulled out a notebook. I caught a glimpse of a magnifying glass, a compass, and little clip things that looked like calipers. Archaeology tools. The guy wrote down the directions, thanked us, and then hurried into the market.

"I can't believe we just met a real live ghost hunter," said T. J.

"He wasn't a ghost hunter," I said. "He was an archaeologist. Didn't you see his T-shirt?"

"You can't believe everything you read on a T-shirt, Fish," said Roger. "Think of all the first-grade Jedi warriors there would be in the world."

"I know," I said. "But he had archaeology equipment."

"That was ghost-hunting equipment," said T. J.

"A magnifying glass is for studying artifacts—"

"No, it's for studying ectoplasm," said T. J. "The stuff that ghosts are made of."

"Give me a break, Teej," I said. "He had calipers for measuring objects and a compass for noting the coordinates at a dig site. You scared the guy off with your ghost mumbo jumbo."

"Yep, Teej. You really spooked him," Roger said. "Get it?"

"He was just nervous about the ghost," said T. J. "Even the professionals on the show get nervous. But he had the right gear. A thermometer to find the cold spots, and—"

"That wasn't a thermometer—" I began.

"Dudes, please!" said Roger. "I scream, you scream, we all scream for—"

"Ice cream!"

After I had recycled a bunch more bottles and cans, I let Roger have a turn.

"Wonder what that ghost-hunting guy was doing in the market," said T. J.

"That's just what I was wondering," I said.

"Doing what everybody else does in the market," said Roger. "Getting food."

"What kind of food do you think a ghost hunter eats?"

"BOO-berries, of course," said Roger, his brown eyes crinkling.

T. J. and I both laughed even though it was a cheesy joke.

"And if he's an archaeologist, you know what he eats? *Past*achio ice cream. Get it? *Past*achio, like an archaeologist digs up stuff from the—"

"Oh, brother," I said as an idea formed in my mind. "Hey, let's go see."

"See what he eats?" said T. J., blowing a big bubble with his gum even though it was peppermint and not bubble gum. I swear he can blow bubbles out of anything.

"No, why an archaeologist would be going to Raven Hill—"

"Or a ghost hunter," said T. J.

"Or a ghost-hunting archaeologist," said Roger, popping another can in the machine.

"Let's tail him," I said.

T. J. and I started in the first aisle. Produce. No sign of the guy. Next we tried hot and cold cereal and coffee. No luck. Detergent and paper products. Nothing. We were just about to walk past the jumbo packages of toilet paper on display at the end of that aisle and try the pasta and international foods aisle when we heard a loud, grouchy old-lady voice say, "No air? What does that have to do with Benedict Billings buying the old Royce place?"

I held up my hand to stop T. J.

"No hair?" said the grouchy voice again. "Benedict Bill-ings isn't bald."

"No HEIR," said a woman's voice that sounded familiar.

"Why didn't you say so?"

I stuck my head out from behind the toilet paper to see who was talking. The grouchy voice belonged to old Mrs. Osborn, Two O's great-grandma. She was leaning on her cane, her hair in a white pouf on top of her head like a Q-tip, with a big frown on her face. Two O says Great-Grandma O is really tough for ninety-six, even if she does sometimes put her false teeth in the freezer and her frozen peas in the medicine cabinet.

She was talking to Ms. Valen, who is in charge of the Special Collection at the library.

"Sad place, that house," went on Great-Grandma Osborn. "Full of secrets even when Thomas Royce and I were children."

"You and Admiral Thomas Royce were friends, Mrs. Osborn?" said Ms. Valen. A copy of today's edition of the *Whooping Hollow Star* poked out of her shopping basket. She loves history, especially local history.

Great-Grandma Osborn didn't answer. "All the whispers about the people who came and went there in the old days and disappeared."

"Do you mean the Underground Railroad?" said Ms. Valen. "I believe Hannibal Royce, the whaler who built the house, was an abolitionist."

"He built the cemetery, too, with just the one gravestone for her. We got into a lot of trouble when we found it."

"Cemetery?" said Ms. Valen.

"In the pines," said old Mrs. Osborn. "So overgrown with pricker bushes we got all scratched up. Never would have found it if it hadn't been for Thomas's new puppy. It got lost, you see. All those years ago, I can still see that puppy now. A little terrier it was, named Jip."

HOLY CANNOLI! A secret cemetery at the one-legged whaler's house?

"Who was buried there?" asked Ms. Valen.

"Buried where?"

"In the pines," Ms. Valen reminded her. "At the Hannibal Royce—"

"His wife, of course," said Great-Grandma Osborn.

"But his wife is buried beside him at the Old Whalers Cemetery," said Ms. Valen.

"That's right," said Great-Grandma Osborn. "His *second* wife is buried there."

"But Hannibal Royce only had one wife," said Ms. Valen.

"It was a small stone with an angel engraved on it," said Great-Grandma Osborn, as if she hadn't heard Ms. Valen. Maybe she hadn't, since Two O said she refused to wear her hearing aid.

"There were yellow rosebushes planted all around it."

"Perhaps you are confusing Hannibal Royce with Nathan Royce, Thomas Royce's father, who inherited the house. Nathan was married twice. I was just researching the family tree. But they were all buried in the cemetery in town."

"He was a wild one, Thomas Royce," said Great-Grandma Osborn, talking to herself. "Full of dreams and plans. When the war came, he went off with the others. That was the end for him. Oh, he survived, but he was never the same."

"You really think there was a cemetery—" said Ms. Valen, trying to get Great-Grandma O back on topic.

"Where would I find the frozen peas?"

So Two O wasn't kidding about the peas. I hoped she put them in the freezer this time.

"In the last aisle, next to the ice cream," said Ms. Valen, pointing. "About the cemetery . . ."

FAMILY TREE

A chart that gives an overview of a family as far back as the records go, linking all family members. It can start with the current generation (you) and go back to your great-great-great-grandparents and beyond, as far back as your family can be researched.

"Cemetery? What cemetery? *Pshaw!*" With that, Great-Grandma O hobbled away on her cane.

"KA-CHING! KA-CHING!" Roger called.

T. J. and I both jumped and knocked into the tower of toilet paper rolls.

WHOOSH! PHWOMP! AAAHHH!

"Boys!" Ms. Valen hurried over as toilet paper rolls landed all around us.

Believe it or not, Roger, T. J., and I are friends with Ms. Valen. We kind of accused her of being part of this plot to steal Captain Kidd's treasure. We wound up finding the treasure, which wasn't gold or jewels or anything fancy. It was mostly old papers, which librarians love, especially librarians who archive stuff about local history, like Ms. Valen. To her it really was treasure.

"Do you think there's really a cemetery at the one-legged whaler—I mean the old Royce house?" I asked, as we restacked the toilet paper.

"So you were listening?" said Ms. Valen, raising one dark eyebrow.

T. J. and I both blushed.

"Sorry," I said.

"It's good to see young people who care about the history of this town," Ms. Valen said. "And I know you boys do."

"If there was a secret cemetery, that could explain the haunting," said T. J.

"Haunting?" said Ms. Valen.

"Secret cemetery?" said Roger.

I shook my head at him to keep quiet as T. J. said, "The entity haunting the one-legged whaler's house that needs to be set free."

"Quit the ghost talk, Teej," I said.

"I've heard mention of a cemetery," said Ms. Valen. "But no one has ever discovered it. I think in part because it was just considered to be a spooky story. One local historian, who is writing a book about the Underground Railroad in the North, is convinced it's because runaway slaves were hidden there and then helped on their way north to Canada. She thinks Hannibal Royce encouraged the idea of the hidden cemetery to scare people off, not because anyone was really buried there."

"Do you think Hannibal Royce was married twice?" I asked.

Ms. Valen shrugged. "No proof has ever been found of that, either. And even if he was, that doesn't mean they had children. Since Admiral Thomas Royce is dead and there is no heir to inherit, it does seem as if the house will be sold. All that history. Gone."

After she walked away, Roger looked at us, jingling the change in his pockets. "Time to *I scream*?" he said. "Hey, did you ever find the ghost-hunting archaeologist?"

T. J. and I shook our heads.

"Tartar Sauce!!!" I said, realizing that our eavesdropping had made us lose track of our suspect. "He's probably long gone by now."

HANNIBAL WELCOME ROYCE — FAMILY TREE
·KNOWN BRANCH·

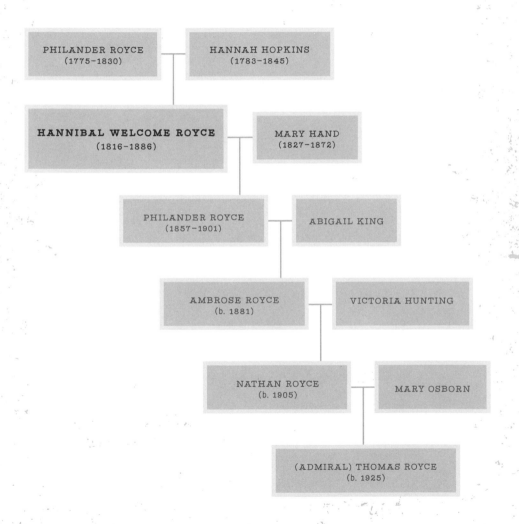

PHILANDER ROYCE
(1775–1830)

HANNAH HOPKINS
(1783–1845)

HANNIBAL WELCOME ROYCE
(1816–1886)

MARY HAND
(1827–1872)

PHILANDER ROYCE
(1857–1901)

ABIGAIL KING

AMBROSE ROYCE
(b. 1881)

VICTORIA HUNTING

NATHAN ROYCE
(b. 1905)

MARY OSBORN

(ADMIRAL) THOMAS ROYCE
(b. 1925)

"Well, what are we waiting for?"

We split up and looked all over the market, but there was no sign of him. I was right. He was long gone.

"Now, what's up with this secret cemetery?" asked Roger.

T. J. and I filled him in about the conversation between Ms. Valen and Great-Grandma O. We were still talking about the secret cemetery when we finally got our ice cream. As it turned out, we did have money for three double-scoop cones with two toppings each. Roger was right.

"See, Great Brain," said Roger. "Sometimes it's not about calculating anything. It's about being a good guesser."

"In math that's called estimating," I said as I took a lick of my cookies-and-cream cone with chocolate and multicolored sprinkles.

"You really think there's a secret cemetery at the one-legged whaler's house?" T. J. asked for the millionth time.

"*Guess* we'll find out," said Roger.

We had agreed it was a good idea to do a bike-by and reconnaissance mission to see what we'd be up against Saturday night.

"Dr. Ghost B. Gone always says, 'It pays to be prepared,'" said T. J., sucking the ice cream out of the bottom of his cone.

"Hey, that's what you always say, too, Fish," said Roger. "Looks like you and the doc have something in common."

"I doubt it," I said. "How do you mean prepared, T. J.?"

"Don't worry. I'll bring everything we need," he said as we came to Red Fox Lane and his house. "See you tomorrow."

"Don't you mean TOMBmorrow?" said Roger. "Get it— TOMBmorrow?!"

A-HAUNTING WE WILL GO

"What are you doing?" I yelled the next afternoon. Roger had tipped over the Huckletons' trash can that he had just put out for garbage pickup.

"And now for a feat that defies the imagination," Roger said. "I will ollie over this great green ginormous gigan—"

"Garbage can," I said with a grin.

Roger skateboarded down the curb in front of my house into the street. When he got to the CAUTION: DUCKS CROSSING sign at the end, he turned around and headed back fast, aiming for the garbage can. At the very last second, when I was sure he was going to crash, he ollied up and over it— don't ask me how—flipped around in midair, and landed on the board.

At the same moment, a delivery truck turned down the street.

"Wonder who's the lucky duck," said Roger as we pushed the can out of the street.

The truck went right past my house. Oh, well. And past Roger's house, too. Then it stopped and backed up. The Huckletons' front door flew open and Summer, Roger's older sister, ran down the steps, wobbling like crazy. She had on high heels and one of those floppy French hats called berets. She still beat Roger to the truck, though. She smiled at the driver as she signed for the package.

"Merci," she said.

The driver just looked at her.

"That's French for thank you," she said.

"Je t'aime, Beck!" Roger made fake smooching sounds.

Since *je t'aime* means *I love you*, I knew it was sure to make Summer mad, since she's got a humongous crush on Beck Billings, Bryce's older brother. He and Summer and a bunch of middle-school kids are studying French this summer. They have French pen pals and learn all about life in France even though they're not going to go there for years, not until high school.

"Fermez la bouche!" said Summer. It's the French way of saying shut your trap, I think. "Or I'll tell Mom you were doing skating tricks in the street again and you'll . . ." Her voice trailed off. "It's for you. It must be a late birthday present." She tossed the package to Roger, who caught it with a loud whoop.

One look at the box and he frowned and threw it onto the grass.

"Hi, guys," called T. J., biking up to us, a bulging shopping bag hanging off his handlebars. "I brought everything we need."

"Aren't you going to open your package?" I asked.

Roger shrugged and started ollieing up and down the curb.

"I love packages," said T. J. "Who's it from?"

I bent down to look at the box. It was dented pretty bad, as if it had traveled a long way. There was no return address, but there were a bunch of stamps in different colors with words in languages that weren't English.

"I bet it's from his dad," I said.

Roger's dad writes about extreme sports. His job takes him all over the world, which means he's not home all that much.

Roger's mom and dad just got divorced. His dad didn't make it home for Roger's birthday last week because he was in Tibet, covering a story about a famous mountain climber. He didn't call, either. I told Roger it was probably because he couldn't get a signal from up on the mountain, but Roger said it didn't matter if his dad called or not, 'cause he didn't care. That wasn't true. Roger missed his dad and he cared a lot.

"I wonder what's in the package," said T. J.

Roger's dad always gives Roger the most awesome presents.

"I guess since Roger doesn't want his package, that means we can have it, T. J.," I said in a loud voice, giving T. J. a wink. It was kind of sneaky, but reverse psychology always works on my little sister, Feenie.

"Yup," said T. J. "Finders keepers."

"I bet I can open it with my scissors," I said, pulling out my pocketknife, which had lost the knives long before Grandpa Finelli gave it to me. You would be surprised how much you can do with a spoon and scissors.

I was just about to cut through the tape when Roger swiped the box out of my hands. "Hey, that's mine."

"So open it!"

Roger grabbed the scissors and ripped open the box. Inside was another box labeled TROPHY CAM SPY Z99-IRXT.

"'See who wanders into your backyard at night with the D55 infrared flash camera, which shoots up to three photos per second while you sleep. . . .'" Roger read from the back of the box.

"Wow!" said T. J. "We could put it up in a tree to see if there's a panther in the neighborhood."

"Panthers are not even native to the United States," I said. "The only large black cats in the U.S. are jaguars. They lived in the Southwest until they were killed off by ranchers in the late nineteenth century."

"Burt Babinski said there was a panther loose in the woods a few years ago, and the police went after it with shotguns," said T. J.

"That's a tall tale," I said. "You know, like Paul Bunyan freezing the Whistling River and pulling it straight. Remember from English class? Anyway, it was probably just a big black dog and somebody mistook it for a panther."

Roger opened the box and took out the camera, which was decorated with a camo pattern. He put his eye to the lens and trained it around my yard.

"With my infrared vision, I see a panther right over there in the deep dark pine trees—"

"That's it! It's just what we need." T. J. opened his shopping bag. "I got a recorder in case there are any EVPs, and—"

PAUL BUNYAN

A giant lumberjack who was the hero of tall tales told round the campfire at lumber camps. Stories were first published in 1910 about how he created famous landmarks like the Great Lakes and the Grand Canyon, and how his camp stove was an acre long. Believed to be based on Fabian Fournier (also called Saginaw Joe), a Canadian lumberjack.

"What's an EVP?" I shouldn't have asked.

"Electronic Voice Phenomena," said T. J. "That's when an entity speaks."

"Oooh!" said Roger. "Ghost talk. Spooky!"

"And I brought a thermometer to check for cold spots, but Dr. Ghost B. Gone says an IR camera—you know, infrared, like the one you just got, Rog—is critical in a—"

"Ghost hunt," said Roger, grinning.

"This isn't a ghost hunt," said T. J.

"Then what is it?" said Roger. "A fright fest? A haunted horror?

A creepy . . ." He paused, trying to think of something creepy that started with *C*.

"It's a paranormal investigation," said T. J.

"Oh, brother," I said, shaking my head.

"We don't know what kind of haunting we might be facing," said T. J. "It could just be an orb, which is the most common kind of entity and isn't dangerous. Or ectoplasm, which is a smoky mist and can be yucky. Or a streak or a shadow person, or worst of all, an elemental."

"Cut the ghost talk, okay, because I am telling you there is no ghost," I said. "It's a bike-by and reconnaissance mission. We need to do a perimeter check that may or may not involve actually breaching the target."

"I hope you're right and we don't encounter an entity, Fish," said T. J. in a calm voice, as if he knew something I didn't. "But like you always say, we have to be prepared. I think I should be the head field investigator because I know the most about paranormal stuff. Then our team needs—"

"Team?" I raised my eyebrows.

"Yes. Our paranormal investigation team needs a technical expert and an interviewer."

"Interviewer?" Roger's brown eyes twinkled.

"Uh-huh. Someone has to make contact with the entity and get it to tell us what it wants and why it's haunting the house in the—"

"That's me," said Roger. "I can talk to anyone. My mom says I would even talk to a blinking light."

"Good," said T. J. "So, you want to be the technical specialist, Fish? The tech guy always carries the EMF meter on the show. Think your dad has one? I looked around, but my dad doesn't. I guess you don't need EMF meters in waste management."

EMF meters detect fluctuations in the electromagnetic field on the electromagnetic spectrum. My dad and Uncle Norman use one sometimes to measure the electromagnetic field at a job site to make sure the wiring is safely installed when they're plumbing new pipes.

"Dr. Ghost B. Gone says if the readings go up and down a lot, it means there's a ghost—I mean an entity—present," said T. J.

"My dad has a meter, but it doesn't matter, because there is no ghost at the one-legged whaler's house, because there are no such things as ghosts."

"That's what the EMF meter will tell us," said T. J.

I shook my head and sighed.

"Do you think the ghost would prefer I speak very proper and say something like 'Salutations on this fine morning, Your Honorable Manifestation'? Or would it feel more comfortable with a casual tone like, 'Yo! Wassup, spirit dude?'" said Roger.

"Guys, you know there's a scientific explanation for anything we might find," I said.

"Dr. Ghost B. Gone says ghosts exist outside the realm of science—" T. J. began again.

"I'd like to tell Dr. Ghost B. Gone a few things," I muttered.

"You can call him," said T. J. "He says at the end of every show: 'Got a haunting going on? Call 1-555-GOS-TBGN . . . '"

FA·BOO·LOUS!!!

"Let's go, guys," I said, checking my digital diver's watch. "It's almost two and I have to be home by four to mow the lawn."

As if she had supersonic hearing, my mom called out the kitchen window, "Fish, don't forget to mow the lawn!"

"I won't, Mom! Be back soon."

Roger, T. J., and I headed down the driveway before my mom could ask where we were going. It wasn't as if we weren't allowed to go to Raven Hill Road, but if my mom asked why, it would be hard to explain, since I couldn't tell her about the dare.

"Are you sure you really need the princess recorder?" I asked T. J. as the shopping bag on his handlebars clanked his tire spokes with each turn of the wheel. This made the pink plastic recorder with pictures of princesses all over it pop up and the pink microphone peek out of the bag, so T. J. had to keep pushing it back down. It belonged to Mmm, T. J.'s little sister, who is princess-crazy, like my four-year-old sister, Feenie.

"It's for Roger's interview."

Roger bowed and somehow popped a wheelie at the same time. "How about: 'Roger Huckleton here, Paranormal Interviewer, to ask you a few SPOOKtacular questions. . . .'"

"It's also to record EVPs," T. J. went on. "That's noise that sounds like static, but if we play it back and run it through a computer the way Dr. Ghost B. Gone's team does, we might hear a message from the entity."

"Sounds faBOOlous!" said Roger.

"What do you need the detective kit for?" I asked.

"We should take a sample of the blood on the door to analyze in our lab."

"What lab?"

"Your lab. You have all that chemistry equipment and the microscope you got for your birthday last year."

"Dude, when are you going to get it through your head there are no such things as ghosts and bleeding doors?"

FISH FINELLI: GHOSTS DON'T WEAR GLASSES

"You'll see, Fish," said T. J. "The EMF meter will show us."

"It's not going to tell us anything other than the level of electromagnetic radiation coming from the power lines and—"

"Hey, Teej," said Roger. "What are the types of ghosts again? I want to be prepared for my interview."

"I can't believe you're taking this seriously," I said as we biked over the railroad tracks into town. "There is absolutely no proof ghosts exist."

"Actually, there is," said T. J. "But it's like meteors."

"What in the heck do meteors have to do with ghosts?" I said.

"They're both out of this world," said Roger.

"See, scientists never used to believe that meteors existed, either, because they didn't fall very often. Just like ghosts. They don't appear all that often, and when they do, you can't just make them appear again. Presto!"

That was just about the most unscientific scientific explanation I had ever heard. I was about to say so when we passed the library and reached Town Pond.

"Shortcut up Pudding Hill, or the long way along Harbor Road?"

"Pudding Hill," T. J. and I both said.

Supposedly during the Revolutionary War, when a British officer came to the door of one house, the woman who lived there threw a pudding at him. That's how the road got its name. It's a steep hill, but it's worth the climb.

When we got to the top, it was just a few turns till we reached Raven Hill Road. It was quiet. It didn't seem like there was anyone around.

We pedaled slowly up to the one-legged whaler's house, where Raven Hill ended.

A dead end.

It was a sunny afternoon, but the Hannibal Royce house sat in shadow, like the light got sucked up by all the overgrown trees and wild grass. The rusty, spiked, black wrought-iron fence looked like a mouth with teeth missing.

The house was set back down a long, winding driveway. It was three stories, gray from the ancient, peeling paint, and an old bent weather vane stuck up at the top. There were two crumbling chimneys that looked like they might collapse at any minute.

T. J. held his shopping bag as if it were a life preserver. Mi was right: If ghosts existed, this house was just the kind of creepy place where they would live.

"Let's leave our bikes here," I said. "And evaluate the entrances and exits so we know what we're doing tomorrow night."

I went first through the rusty fence, wading slowly through the tall grass. No one had lived here for a long, long time. Even when Admiral Thomas Royce—Hannibal Royce's great-great-great-I-don't-know-how-many-greats-grandson—was alive, no one came here. He was a recluse—you know, someone who doesn't like to be around other people, even people he used to be friends with when he was a kid, like Great-Grandma Osborn.

The only person I know who had ever been here was the Captain. I think they were friends on account of having both been in World War II. Admiral Royce died more than ten years ago, before I was born, and the house was just sitting here, left to rot.

CRACK!

Something crashed through the bushes ahead of us. We froze in our tracks.

"What was that?" whispered Roger.

We had reached a bend in the driveway where a giant weeping willow tree blocked the house from view. My heart

rat-tat-tatted in my chest, but all I could see was a green curtain of leaves.

WHOOSH!

Something black darted through the leaves over our heads.

A raven.

We rounded the willow and saw the house in front of us. We spotted the ravens everywhere—by the front porch, by the side porch, up in the tree. They all looked at us at the same time with their beady black eyes.

"What do ravens eat?" whispered T. J., so close to me I could feel his breath in my ear.

"They're carrion birds, so they eat things that are dead," I said.

At the word *dead*, the three of us looked at one another. A second later, the ravens flapped their big black wings and disappeared into the trees.

"Guess it's not called Raven Hill for nothing," said Roger.

The house had a wide front porch and a side porch that both had skinny versions of those columns with curlicues on the top. I think they are called Ionic. The wooden steps were rotted, and shutters were missing or hanging at weird angles off all the windows. I had to admit the place sure was creepy.

"Let's see if the front door is unlocked," I said, trying to sound braver than I felt. "That will be the easiest way for us to get in on Saturday night."

I went first, then Roger, then T. J. There were dark brownish-reddish streaks running down the side of the door.

"Holy cannoli!" said Roger.

"Oh, jeepo!" said T. J. "The door really is bleeding."

I swallowed hard. "We . . . don't know if that's really . . . uh . . . blood."

"Take out the EMF meter," said T. J. "To measure the level of paranormal activity."

"Why are you whispering? I bet it's only rust," I said, but my heart thumped fast.

I pulled out the EMF meter and flipped it on. T. J. and Roger crowded around to see. At first nothing happened, but then I moved it an inch closer to the door. The needle on the display jumped all the way from two hertz at the bottom to one hundred and twenty hertz at the top and then back down again. I moved it an inch closer and it did the same wild swing from top to bottom. An inch closer. This time the needle went to the top and stayed there.

"So, Teej, that means there's a gho—I mean an entity in the house, right?" said Roger.

T. J. just nodded, his face so pale, all his freckles stood out.

"It might not be an elementary thingy like the one you said was bad. It might be one of those friendlier ones that just lights up or bangs a door or floats around in a smoky mist, right?"

Roger tends to talk a lot when he's scared. It was up to me to stay calm. *There are no such things as ghosts. . . . There are no such things as ghosts. . . .*

"I bet it's just a power line that's making the meter go crazy," I said, which made sense now that I said it out loud. "Or some messed-up wiring. Let's . . . um . . . see if the door is open."

Roger and T. J. took a step back as I reached for the doorknob. I pushed once before I lost my nerve. It didn't budge. No spooky orb or streak or ghost lunged out to get us, either, so I tried again, leaning my shoulder into the door. No luck.

"Guess we should try another door," I said.

I led the way around the side of the house. We had to push through a nasty tangle of dead rosebushes. They were all thorns and I pricked myself a bunch of times. The side

EMF METER

EMF, or electromagnetic fields, are invisible lines of force that surround an electrical device. They are caused by the motion of an electric charge. An EMF meter is a scientific instrument used to measure electromagnetic fields that come from sources like electric wiring, power lines, and appliances. Their unit of measurement is called a hertz (Hz).

porch steps were so rotten, the middle one had collapsed.

"Watch your step," I said, jumping over it.

"There's blood on this door, too," whispered T. J., as he and Roger walked slowly up the steps behind me. "See it dripping over there?" He pointed to the line of brownish-reddish drip marks.

"I bet it's a combination of rust from the door hinges and sap from the trees. That's why it's on both doors." With so many trees hanging over the house, it was possible.

"Hmm," said Roger, a relieved look on his face. "I think you're *dead* right."

Now that Roger was back to making wisecracks and I had come up with a logical explanation, I wasn't afraid to try the side door. I pushed hard on the knob, but this door didn't budge, either.

"I think it's locked, too." I wiggled the knob.

"Be careful, Fish," said T. J. "You don't want to alarm the entity."

"For Pete's sake," I said, shoving the door with my shoulder to see what would happen. It creaked, and I felt it give. "There's no ghost, T. J. Hey, this door is just stuck. Push it with me."

T. J. and I both pushed. With a loud creak, the door swung open. I caught a glimpse of a refrigerator, which meant this was probably the kitchen.

"Should we go in and see if we can find the harpoon?" I said. "That way we'll be prepared on Saturday night."

No one knew for sure if there really was a harpoon. The one-legged whaler stabbing his victims through the heart with it was just a story, after all. But Hannibal Royce had supposedly left behind a collection of whaling stuff from his days at sea. It had been passed down from generation to generation with the house. The Captain told me Hannibal Royce, besides being a whaler, was also an inventor who patented special harpoons and whale hoists to raise dead whales out of the sea.

"I don't know," said T. J. "I think we should check the EMF meter first."

"T. J., please," I said. "What do you think, Rog?"

There was no answer.

"Roger?" I said again.

T. J. and I turned around. Roger was gone.

"Roger!"

No answer. A raven landed on the grass at the foot of the steps and cawed, its beady black eyes on us.

"AAAHHH!" Roger's scream echoed in the silence.

T. J. gripped his shopping bag so tight, his knuckles turned white. "The ghost got him. . . . "

IT'S AN ORB! IT'S A GHOST! IT'S COMING!

A shiver ran down my spine. T. J. stood frozen beside me, stiff as a Queen's Guard at Buckingham Palace. All he needed was one of those furry black hats and a pair of shiny black boots.

TAP. TAP. TAP. Footsteps echoed from inside.

TAP. TAP. TAP. They were heading this way.

"It's the ghost!" T. J. said, jumping off the porch.

CRRREEEAAAKKK!!! The kitchen door creaked farther open. T. J. was right. The house really *was* haunted.

CRRREEEAAAKKK!!!

I leapt off the porch, landing in a heap beside T. J. "We have to find Roger."

"AAAAHHHH!" We heard another scream.

"We have to help him," I said, getting to my feet. "We'll talk to the ghost just like you said, and uh . . . get it to . . . uh . . . let Roger go."

"BOO!"

The sound echoed in the silence as Roger burst through the kitchen door. "Scared you!"

"Roger!"

"I wasn't scared," I said.

"Were too," said Roger. "You looked as if you'd seen a ghost."

"Ha. Ha. How'd you get in, anyway?"

"There's a window on the other side of the porch that was boarded up, and one of the boards was loose," said Roger. "Easy peasy."

"I'll lemon squeezy you," I said, grabbing Roger around the neck.

"I got you guys," said Roger, his eyes twinkling. "Come on. Admit it."

QUEEN'S GUARD

Responsible for guarding the Queen at Buckingham Palace and St. James's Palace in London, foot guards wear red tunics and black bearskin hats that are eighteen inches tall and weigh one and a half pounds. They shoulder arms and stand for ten minutes and then march up and down before returning to position. If someone steps in front of them they say, "Make way for the Queen's Guard."

I shook my head and changed the subject. "So, T. J., since you're the lead investigator, shouldn't you go first?"

T. J. nodded, still pale. "I think you should turn on the EMF detector, Fish."

"I'm telling you, the only ghost around here is Roger, and he doesn't look very ghostly to me."

T. J., still unconvinced, led the way through the doorway, holding his shopping bag like a shield. It was kind of dim, so I pulled out my pocket flashlight. I trained the narrow light on an old wooden table, old cane-back chairs seated around it, cabinets, and a stove. The sink was the old-fashioned kind with those enamel-topped faucets, one for hot and one for cold, that my dad and Uncle Norman complain need new washers all the time on account of the iron content in the well water eroding the metal. A thick layer of dust and cobwebs covered everything.

PLINK! PLINK!

"What was that?" asked T. J.

"The faucet," I said. "Nothing to worry about."

We walked through a swinging door into another room with a longer wooden table and more chairs.

"Dining room," said Roger.

"No harpoon here," said Roger, coughing from the dust.

"No ghost, either," I said. "See, T. J.?"

The next door led us into a wide hallway. To our right was the front door. Opposite was a sweeping set of stairs leading to the upper floors. Across from us were two doors that were closed.

There was a grandfather clock in one corner and a few small tables and chairs covered in sheets on top of a faded, worn-out Oriental rug. The ceiling was high, made of dark wood paneling, and a chandelier hung from the very top, covered in cobwebs. The way it tilted to one side, I sure hoped it wouldn't fall.

"No harpoon here," said Roger. "Man, these are the biggest dust bunnies ever. AAHH-CHOO!"

"Maybe we should try one of the rooms over there." I shined the flashlight on the two closed doors. The longer we stayed in the house, the more confident I felt.

"Guys . . . ," said T. J. "I feel a cold spot. Watch out, because a cold spot means the entity is sucking up all the heat and electricity and stuff so it can manifest. If it's a really powerful ghost, it can suck out all the charge in electronic devices, like your flashlight or phone."

"T. J., I'm telling you there is no such thing as ghosts."

"I feel it, too, Fish," said Roger, dropping his jokey tone. "T. J.'s right. It is colder here."

I walked over and the three of us stood in a huddle at the foot of the staircase. T. J. pulled a white thermometer out of his bag. I bet he got it out of the Jacuzzi tub in his garage, where his dad keeps all the stuff he picks up on carting jobs that he thinks might be useful one day but that his mom doesn't want around.

"Shine the light on this, Fish."

"Seventy-eight degrees," I said. "That's not cold."

"Look!" said Roger. "It's dropping."

"I'm telling you, this is a cold spot." T. J.'s hands shook as he held the thermometer.

We watched the red liquid slowly drop from seventy-eight down to seventy-four and then seventy. A cool breeze prickled the hairs on the back of my neck.

"It's a draft, guys," I said, sweeping my flashlight around.

"How can there be a draft?" said Roger. "The whole place is shut up."

"See, when even a little cool air enters through a window or a door, objects lose heat in an attempt to equalize room temperature. The process is called convection, and because hot air rises—"

All of a sudden, my flashlight went out.

"Jeepo!" said T. J.

I jiggled my flashlight, but it wouldn't go back on.

"The entity sucked up all the charge," said T. J.

"What's that mean?" said Roger, his voice quavering.

"It's trying to . . . manifest," whispered T. J. "You know, turn into a gh-gh-ghost."

We blinked in the sudden dimness, waiting for our eyes to adjust. I was about to pop out the batteries to switch them around when a floating light appeared at the top of the stairs.

"It's an orb!"

BANG! A door slammed somewhere nearby.

"It's a poltergeist!"

A shadowy form appeared where the light had been.

"It's a shadow being!"

The shadow started moving toward the stairs with a THUMP! THUMP! THUMP!

"It's the ghost of the one-legged whaler!"

"It's coming!"

1·555·GOS·TBGN

We ran out of the house so fast, we didn't stop till we were all the way back down the driveway and had reached the safety of our bikes. We'd gotten scratched up from the thorns and prickers, and Roger had ripped his shorts, but nobody said a word, not till we were safely off Raven Hill Road and on Main Street.

T. J. didn't say I told you so. Roger did, but I knew there had to be a scientific explanation for what had happened. I was still thinking about it even after I finished mowing the lawn.

"I have something important to tell you," said Feenie as soon as I walked into the kitchen. Her blond pigtails bounced up by her ears, but her blue eyes were serious.

"What?" I said, taking a long gulp of cold water. I wiped my sweaty forehead with the bottom of my T-shirt. Mowing was hard work, especially when you used an old-fashioned lawn mower. It was the kind you push that doesn't have a motor. My mom takes being green to a whole new level.

"Two hundred raisins on a hill—AH-CHOO!—April Day," she said.

"Huh?" I said, taking another drink of water. "What kind of riddle is that?"

I was only half listening. I knew the ghost had to be an optical illusion, like magicians create when they pull a coin out of someone's ear. That's what I had told the guys. Because we had ghosts on our minds, our brains tricked us into thinking random shadows were a ghost. What T. J. said was an orb was just a trick of the light shining through a window and reflecting off the chandelier. The banging sounds weren't made by a poltergeist, but just a loose shutter flapping in the wind or a door slamming in the breeze from a broken window. It was harder to explain the shadow being and the thumping sounds, but I knew there had to be a logical explanation for that, too.

"It's not a riddle, silly," said Feenie. "It's a message."

"From who?"

"From *whom*," corrected my mom, waving her wooden spoon.

"The Captain," said Feenie.

"What? The Captain called me?"

The Captain is like another grandpa to me. He lives by Whale Rock, where we dock our boat, the *Fireball*, which used to belong to him before he gave it to me. He was in the Navy for lots of years. Sometimes he shoots off flares and talks in Navy slang. He knows just about everything about boats.

Feenie nodded importantly. "The phone rang, so I went over to the wall right over here." She walked to the phone hanging on the wall by the kitchen table. "And I picked it up." She picked up the receiver. "And I said—"

OPTICAL ILLUSION

This happens when our eyes send information to our brains that tricks us into seeing something that does not match what is really there. Optic nerves at the back of the eye connect to the central nervous system in the brain. The brain receives electrical impulses from our eyes, which is how we see. Sometimes the brain is confused by this information.

"Forget what you said. What did the Captain say?"

Feenie frowned. "Stop *'trupting* me. I said, 'Hello, Finelli residence, Fiona Finelli speaking.'"

"Very good, Feenie," said my mom, smiling as she stirred a big pot of gravy. That's what we call tomato sauce in our family.

"Why do you let her answer the phone?" I asked.

"It's good practice," said my mom.

"But that message makes no sense," I said. "Tell me again, Feenie."

Feenie scrunched up her nose. "He sneezed and said AH-CHOO!—and then he said two hundred raisins on a hill. April Day."

"That can't be right," I said.

"Is so," said Feenie. "It's what he said. I heard it with my very own ears."

"Your very own ears must have heard wrong. Mom, see what I mean? You shouldn't let her answer the phone if she can't get the message right."

"Fish, don't say that. She's trying."

"It is so right," said Feenie again. "Call the Captain if you don't believe me. Now I have to go to Fairy Headquarters for a meeting with the FQ. That's the Fairy Queen, in case you didn't know." Her pink sparkly fairy wings flapped as she ran out the door.

I headed for the phone Feenie had just hung up. Shrimp, my dog, got up from where he was sleeping under the table. He stretched his front and back legs—I swear he's so big, his paws almost reached from one end of the kitchen to the other. He's part Saint Bernard, which I didn't know when I named him. As I dialed the Captain's number, Shrimp licked my hand with his long, slobbery tongue. He does that when he thinks I'm upset. I patted him on the head, listening as the phone rang and rang.

No one answered so I called again, but it just kept on ringing. . . .

+ + +

Tonight was the night—the night of the full moon. The night of the dare. I wanted to bike down to Whale Rock to ask the Captain some questions about Hannibal Royce and his harpoon collection. But before I could go, my dad needed help cleaning out the garage. Then I had to give Shrimp a bath because he had rolled in deer poop. It took a while, not because Shrimp doesn't like baths, but because there is just so much of him to scrub. I let him run through the sprinkler to rinse off, and Feenie wanted to run through, too. I had to watch her while my parents went to the store. Then I was so hot, I decided to get wet myself.

It was late in the afternoon when Roger vaulted over the hedge between our houses. Before he even said hello, he started taking off his button-down shirt and at the same time kicking off his loafers.

"How was Summer's play?"

"I don't know," said Roger.

"What do you mean, you don't know?"

"It was in French, Great Brain, remember? I don't speak French."

"How was Summer?"

"Happy 'cause she got to do a scene with Beck. They were both wearing berets and waving loaves of French bread around."

"Hmm," I said. "How was Beck?"

"He did this great save when Summer tripped in her high heels. Personally, I thought he should have let her fall. He made wearing a beret look kind of okay. He sure is cool compared to his brother, Darth Billings."

The dare was less than six hours away. The sun was long past the halfway point and would soon be heading for the trees. Even though I didn't believe in ghosts, my stomach was in free fall, like when I'm swimming in the ocean and there is a massive wave heading my way that I have to dive under.

"Guys! Guys!"

We turned as T. J. came biking fast down my driveway, red-faced and sweating.

"You have to come right now."

"What?" I said.

T. J. glanced nervously over his shoulder. "Cell phone."

"Cell phone what?"

"Is this one of those weird word associations? Like, you say 'cell phone' and I say 'surfboard'?" asked Roger.

"What does a surfboard have to do with a cell phone?"

"Both things I want that my mom says no way to."

"I got a cell phone," T. J. said in a whisper.

"Your parents got you a cell phone?" said Roger. "No way, dude!"

"Shh!" said T. J., his eyes darting all over the place. "It's not mine."

"You stole a cell phone?"

"No! We need to go to the upstairs bathroom right now."

"What? Why?" I said.

"Is this a new way to play hide-and-seek?" said Roger.

T. J. shook his head. "He's at batting practice and he'll be back in twenty minutes, twenty-five tops. Come on, guys. We have to hurry."

"Who?"

"Mickey," said T. J. "It's his cell phone. I found it in the bathroom."

Roger and I exchanged uneasy glances. Mickey, T. J.'s older brother, wasn't known as a slugger just because he could pound out the home runs.

"Why do we need Mickey's cell phone?" I asked.

"To call Dr. Ghost B. Gone," said T. J. "It costs two-ninety-five per minute, so we can't use our parents' phones or they'll know."

"That's crazy!" I said.

"Mickey will kill you when he finds out!" said Roger.

T. J. shrugged. "Going into that house tonight, whatever Dr. Ghost B. Gone can tell us could make the difference between life and death—plus it'll take Mickey a while to figure it out."

Mickey didn't get the hottest grades in school. He didn't think it mattered, since he planned to get recruited and play in the majors right out of high school.

"I still don't see why we need to—"

"Fish, please. We've got to call. Like you and Dr. Ghost B. Gone always say—"

"It pays to be prepared," said Roger.

Clearly it was no use arguing. We hopped on our bikes and rode over to the Mahoneys'. I had Feenie sit on the handlebar in front of me, since I had to bring her. Let me tell you, it's no fun biking with fairy wings hitting you in the head.

"Quick!" said T. J., running up the stairs.

Roger and I headed after him into the bathroom, while Feenie went straight to Mmm's room. That was good, since the last thing we needed was her blabbing about our secret phone call.

The phone was on the counter next to a squashed and oozing tube of Fruity Tooty toothpaste.

"So, you gonna call, Teej, since you're the lead paranormal investigator?" said Roger.

T. J. looked like he was at the dentist about to get a bunch of cavities filled instead of making one measly phone call. OK, it was on a stolen phone to a celebrity ghost hunter, but still.

"I'll call, Teej," I said. "Then we'll put it on speakerphone."

"We have to be fast. Mickey will be back in like ten minutes."

"We can't be on the phone that long anyway," I said. "That would cost twenty-nine-ninety-five, and no way is whatever Dr. Ghost B. Gone gonna say worth that." I picked up the phone. "What's the number?"

"1-555-GOS-TBGN," said T. J. in a rush.

I punched the buttons, set the phone to speaker, and put it down on the counter. We listened to it ring. All of a sudden, there was a click and then the show's theme music began to play. "Got a haunting going on? Call 1-555-GHOST-BE-GONE!" Roger sang along.

"Quit it, Rog!" I said.

"You have reached the offices of Dr. Ghost B. Gone. To order the Dr. Ghost B. Gone Haunt-Free Special Collection, press one. If you have a billing question or a question about your order, press two. If you want to leave a message for Dr. Ghost B. Gone, press three. If you are experiencing a haunting emergency, press zero."

"We should press three," I said as Roger and T. J. said, "Zero."

Before I could object, Roger had his finger on the zero. "Definitely a haunting emergency."

"Got a haunting going on?" said a deep, dramatic voice I could only assume belonged to Dr. Ghost B. Gone. "Don't be scared. Most entities are simply confused spirits who need help and are coming to you for guidance. To find out, answer these three questions. One: Does the temperature drop in a certain part of your house?"

"Yes!" shouted Roger.

"Shh!" I said, nodding my head in the direction of Mmm's room.

"Two: Do lights appear and disappear that seem to be floating?"

"Yes!" said Roger and T. J.

"Three: Are there noises you can't explain, particularly banging noises?"

"Yes!" said Roger and T. J.

"If you answered yes to any or all of these questions, then you've probably got an entity on your hands. Here's what you need to do. Join hands and tell the entity that you live there now and it is time for the entity to leave and be free. If that doesn't work, leave your phone number at the tone and I, or one of my paranormal investigators, will get back to you. Remember: Walk softly and carry a big flashlight. There is nothing to fear, unless your entity is an elemental, in which case leave the house right now."

The phone beeped.

"Hi, Mr.—I mean, Dr. Ghost B. Gone. We're . . . um, afraid there's an elemental at the one-legged whaler's house in Whooping Hollow," said Roger.

Then two things happened at the very same moment. The front door banged and Feenie blurted out 789-324-8899, our phone number.

"What are you doing in here, Feenie?" I whipped around.

"Timothy Junior, why are there footprints on my brand-new Barely Beige carpeting?" Mrs. Mahoney yelled up the stairs.

There was another loud bang. "I'm home!" called Mickey.

"Oh, jeepo!" gasped T. J.

The four of us dashed out of the bathroom as footsteps pounded up the stairs.

"Hold on there, mister!" we heard Mrs. Mahoney yell. "Take those sneakers off before you put a foot on that carpet."

"Where's my pink princess recorder?" yelled Mmm, her red pigtails bobbing angrily as she reached the top step. "I know you took it."

"They're using it to catch a ghost," said Feenie solemnly. "They just called a big ghosty guy on the phone in the bathroom."

I swear Feenie has a bright future ahead of her in undercover work. She's not even five yet, and she doesn't miss a thing.

Mmm stopped being angry for a minute. "You used Mickey's phone? You are so dead."

"Don't tell, Mmm, please," said T. J. "Here, have some gum. Have the whole pack." He pulled a crumpled pack of Chiclets out of his pocket.

"That'll cost you a dollar," said Mmm. "Plus the gum."

T. J. frowned. "Here's a token from the arcade at the beach."

Mmm shook her head. "I want real money."

Mmm is a tough negotiator. She and Feenie make a crackerjack team.

"Here," said Roger, rooting around in his pocket. He handed Mmm a golden coin.

"That's not a dollar," said Mmm.

"It's a dollar, all right," said Roger.

"Whoo!" said Feenie. "A golden dollar."

"Now super promise you won't tell," said T. J.

"Super promise?" said Roger.

T. J. nodded. "We're not allowed to swear."

"I super promise I won't tell," said Mmm.

"You too, Feenie," I said. "Not a word about ghosts or phones to anybody."

She frowned. "What do I get?"

"I won't tell Mom you used her perfume on your dolls," I said. "And that you made a hole in the screen door with your magic wand."

"How did you know?" Feenie's eyes widened. "OK, I super promise."

Footsteps thundered up the stairs. It wasn't Mrs. Mahoney, that was for sure.

Mmm looked at T. J. "You're lucky I'm not gonna tell or you would be D-E-D." She made a slashing motion with her finger across her neck.

Roger whistled the *Dr. Ghost B. Gone* theme song as T. J. gulped. He nudged T. J. with his shoulder. "Come on, sing along with me: 'Got a haunting going on? Call 1-555-GHOST-BE-GONE!'"

SPOOKY, KOOKY, AND OOKY

"Fish! It's almost time for dinner!" my mom called. "Roger, do you want to stay?"

"Thanks, Mrs. F.," Roger called back.

We ate outside around the picnic table. Uncle Norman and his girlfriend, Venus, were there, too.

"Please pass the meatballs," said Roger for the third time.

"You got a hollow leg, Roger?" asked my father.

"Mrs. F. makes the best meatballs and gravy. They're just so good and meaty."

"Why, thank you, Roger," said my mom.

"Meatballs are usually meaty since their main ingredient is meat," I said.

"Not when my mom makes them," said Roger through a mouthful of meatball. "Then they're tofurkey."

"Turkey, silly," said Feenie. "There's no such thing as a tofurkey."

"There is, but believe me, you will never see a tofurkey go gobble gobble," said Roger just as the phone started ringing inside the house.

"I'll get it!" yelled Feenie, jumping up from the table and dashing across the backyard.

"Oh, brother," I said as the door slammed behind her.

Feenie was back a minute later with a big, goofy smile on her face. She looked right at me. "It's for you. It's a giiirrrrrlllllll!"

"I wonder who it could be," said Roger, wagging his eyebrows as my mom and dad exchanged glances.

I blushed all the way to the roots of my hair, but luckily I had already hopped off the bench before anyone could see. I was pretty sure I knew who it was, which only made me blush even harder.

I cleared my throat and picked up the phone. "Hello."

"Hi, Fish. It's Clementine."

I felt my face turn even redder as I racked my brains trying to think of something clever to say. All I came up with was "Um . . . hi . . ."

"I wanted to wish you good luck tonight," she said. "And um . . ." Now she was saying "um." Her voice trailed off.

She was nervous, too! That made me less nervous, so I said, "What?"

"It's about . . . Bryce."

Bryce? Why in the world was she calling me about him? He was my mortal enemy, who hated my guts more than . . .

"You know, it's not that he doesn't like you," she said. "It's just that he's jealous of you."

"Jealous?!" I almost dropped the phone. "He's the one who tells me over and over how much cooler he is than me 'cause of all his brand-new cool stuff, and how lame and old my stuff is. What in the world do I have that would make him jealous of me?"

"Your dad," said Clementine.

"All he does is make fun of my dad."

"I know. That's because he's jealous 'cause your dad is around. Your dad goes to your games and has dinner with you and teaches you stuff. Bryce's dad is like my dad. He's always working, so he's not there a lot of the time."

"Oh," I said. I realized Clementine had a point. My dad had been a Cub Scout leader when we were little, taught me everything I know about fixing stuff, and he coached Little League on every team I ever played. He barely even missed a practice.

"I just wanted you to . . . um . . . know that," she said. "Good luck and see you later, Fish."

"S'later, Clementine."

Back outside, I took a big bite of spaghetti. Bryce, jealous of me? It sure was hard to believe. I was about to say something to Roger, but the topic of dads was sort of sensitive for him, too.

"It's too bad about the old Royce place," said Venus all of a sudden, looking right at me, like she knew about our plans. All thoughts about dads flew out of my head with her green eyes on me like laser beams.

"Looks like we're in for a new golf course and condos," said my dad.

"Yep," said Uncle Norman. "Since the years of probate are almost up and there's no will, it seems the house will go to the town. And Benedict Billings has done a good job convincing the town board that luxury condos are just what the town needs. Plus, the town will receive whatever millions the real estate king has promised them for the land."

"But probate doesn't end till Friday," said my dad. "So until then, it still belongs to the Royce family. You never know. An heir might pop up."

"That's true," said Uncle Norman. "It's like fishing. You don't get a bite all day—or all night—and then wham! You've got a big one on your line."

"I'm catching the biggest fish tonight. You watch me," said my dad.

"We'll see about that, big brother."

"I heard runaway slaves stopped at that house on their way to freedom," said Venus. "Imagine that? The Underground Railroad ran right through this town."

"That house is a landmark," agreed my mom. "Plus, Hannibal Royce was one of the most famous whaling captains of his day."

WHALING

People have been whaling for thousands of years. American whaling fleets hunted whales near the Atlantic coast and as far away as the Arctic and Antarctic. Whales were harpooned by men in small boats. When a whale was killed, it was tied by the side of the ship, and the skin and blubber were peeled off and boiled down to make oil. U.S. whaling hit its peak in the mid-19th century.

Venus and my mom cleaned up while my dad and Uncle Norman stayed outside, talking about the moon and the tide and fishing. I was busy putting stuff back in the fridge and thinking about the dare and whether we had everything we needed when Venus said, "I feel sorry for the ghost. It's stuck around this long probably to pass along one final message. If the house gets torn down and the ghost doesn't get to take care of unfinished business, it will only be more unhappy."

"How do you know the ghost is unhappy?" asked Roger.

"You can sense it when you drive by the place," said Venus. "It feels so sad."

My mom was biting her lip the way she does when she's not sure what to say.

"You believe in ghosts?" I asked.

"Well, I think some people can sense them and some can't, so it depends on which kind of person you are," said Venus, looking into my eyes again. "But if a ghost has come into your life, then it means it needs your help."

"Yeah?" said Roger. "That's just what T. J. said when we went to the one-legged whaler's—"

I kicked Roger. Luckily my mom was busy washing the dishes and didn't hear him.

"Good luck, boys," said Venus. "The full moon is an auspicious time for ghost hunting."

Roger and I looked at each other, eyes wide. How in the heck did she know?! I didn't think astrologers were mind readers, too.

The sky was streaked pink and orange as the sun started to set. Sixty minutes till go time. I let myself in the back door of Roger's house and ran down the steps to the basement. T. J. was already there, laying out his sleeping bag. We had planned to sleep over at Roger's since Mrs. Huckleton was going to a late yoga class. That meant we wouldn't have to be home till 9:25. Our curfews are nine o'clock, but when Summer is in charge, so long as we don't bug her, we can pretty much do what we want.

"Let's do an equipment check," said T. J.

"Don't tell me you brought all that crazy Dr. Ghost B. Gone stuff," I said.

T. J. ignored me. "I have the princess recorder and the thermometer. Did you bring the EMF detector?"

I nodded and pulled it out, along with the other much more useful stuff I had in my pockets. "I have my pocketknife, a compass, a flashlight with brand-new batteries, string, a notebook, a pen, and a mini screwdriver. "

"So long as you have the EMF detector, we're okay. It could save our lives."

"Not another matter of life and death," I groaned.

"It's death and death," said Roger, grinning. "And it's the only way I'm gonna know when my subject arrives on the scene so I can start my SPOOKtacular interview."

I shook my head, but I had to laugh. "You know that's ridiculous. No matter what Venus says, I don't believe in ghosts."

"What did Venus say?" asked T. J.

Roger started telling T. J. about the ghost's unfinished business when he stuck his hand in his big cargo shorts pocket and it went right through. "Hey, where's my camera? I know I put it in my pocket."

We looked all over, but we couldn't find it. Stuff like that never bothers Roger, but it was a gift from his dad. No matter what he says, I know that makes it extra special for him.

"It must have fallen out when we ran out of the one-legged whaler's house," said T. J.

"Don't worry," I said. "We'll find it tonight."

"Hey, did you leave it turned on?"

"Yup," said Roger. "It'll be dead as a doornail now."

"Doornails were never alive, so they can't die," I said.

"Will you guys please stop talking about dying?" said T. J. "What is important is that the camera recorded everything. Dr. Ghost B. Gone's team always leaves an IR camera running during a preliminary investigation, to monitor the entity."

My stomach turned over again in that weird roller-coaster way. Maybe that third helping of spaghetti and meatballs wasn't such a good idea.

"We have to go," I said, pushing all ghostly thoughts out of my mind.

It was almost eight o'clock by the time we got to the one-legged whaler's house. The whole place was filled with shadows. The sky was a dark pinky red. At least it was still light out, because the sun didn't set till 8:18.

There was a group of kids gathered in front of the fence, waiting for us. We biked slowly down the road toward them.

"Thought you were going to chicken out," said Bryce, who sat on a brand-new neon-yellow electric scooter.

"Bawk! Bawk!" said Trippy and True.

I was about to get mad at Bryce, but I remembered my conversation with Clementine. It was hard to believe he was jealous of me, sitting on top of that cool new scooter.

Clementine stepped out from behind them. She leaned toward me and whispered, "Good luck!"

"Thanks," I said.

"Good luck, dudes!" Mi and Si fist-bumped us.

Two O said, "Hope you make it out alive, guys. I said a prayer for you."

We stared up at the house and all those overgrown trees. Even Bryce looked uneasy, his eyes darting all over the place.

"So, you losers ready?"

Jealous or not, Bryce was still mean. And that made me forget all about being scared.

"We're not losers, we're ghost hunters," I said.

A murmur went through the crowd.

"You mean paranormal investigators," said T. J.

"Just call us Spooky, Kooky, and Ooky," said Roger.

"And we were born ready," I added, to get into the spirit of things.

The crowd started to cheer. OK, it was the quietest cheer you ever heard, but it was still a cheer.

Then the three of us did our secret handshake and walked through the opened gate and into the trees. . . .

THE GAMMA-RAY GHOST

"Kooky, Spooky, and Ooky?" I said as we made our way along the winding driveway.

"Yeah," said Roger. "T. J. is Spooky because of his paranormal know-how, I'm Kooky 'cause of my crazy and brilliant ideas, and you're Ooky."

"Why am I Ooky?"

"'Cause that's all that's left."

We reached the turn in the driveway at the willow tree. If the one-legged whaler's place was dim and spooky during the day, those shadows were way longer and way darker at sunset, with the last of the light filtering through the leaves. It was hard not to imagine someone or something was hiding in the bushes ready to jump out at us.

We were far from the crowd of kids, and their voices had faded away. Would they hear us if we called for help? I took a deep breath. *It's just an old house. There are no such things as ghosts. The trees are just trees, not shadowy beings with arms reaching out to grab us.*

SCRITCH! SCRATCH! TAP! TAP! SCRITCH! SCRATCH! TAP! TAP!

"What was that?" whispered Roger.

"Just the diurnals on their way to bed and the nocturnals getting ready for the night," I said, rubbing my palms on my shorts.

"Huh?" said T. J.

"You know, the animals that are active during the day, like squirrels and rabbits, are going to bed, and the night animals, like raccoons, are—"

"And bats," said Roger. "I bet there are lots of bats. And you know there's this bat called a vampire bat that sucks human blood and one time one got into this guy's house and bit him in the toe and sucked out all his—"

"Vampire bats only live in South America," I said. "There are none in Whooping Hollow 'cause it's way too cold here."

Our voices trailed off as we found ourselves facing the house. The sun had sunk below the trees and the sky was the deep purple of twilight, with a scattering of stars. Soon the moon would rise. Shadows stretched from where we stood to the house, inky black like long fingers of darkness. The windows with the broken shutters looked out at us like empty eyes.

"It sure is dark," said T. J.

I pulled out my flashlight and turned it on. Somehow the little light it cast only made the dark all around us seem even darker. And that made the rustlings and creakings seem even louder.

"Guys," whispered T. J. in a quavering voice, his flashlight shaking in his hand. "You know entities feed off fear, so it's important not to get scared."

"I'm not scared," said Roger in a squeaky voice, turning on his light.

I led the way up to the house. We stopped a few feet from the porch and we all looked up at the door.

"Think the house has been bleeding since we left?" said Roger.

"Knock it off, Roger. Those drip marks are exactly the same as they were before. And they're dry." I shined my flashlight on them to prove my point. "See? Let's get going. We only have an hour before we need to get home. We should retrace our steps to the main hallway and then try the rooms across from the dining room. Maybe one of them is the study."

"You think someone would keep a harpoon in a study?" said Roger.

"Maybe," I said. "Hannibal Royce collected harpoons, besides inventing them. Lots of times people keep collections of old valuable stuff in a study, so it's possible that's what Admiral Royce did with his ancestor's harpoons."

"It might be in the basement," said T. J. "You know, where everyone says the ghost—I mean, the entity—put its victims."

"Think we're going to find the skeleton of the paperboy down there?" said Roger. "Wonder if his ghost wanders around, too. . . ."

BEEP! BEEP! We all jumped.

"It's just my watch, guys," I said. "I set it to go off every fifteen minutes, so we won't lose track of time." None of us wanted to get home late and be grounded. "Let's go. It's eight o'clock on the dot."

"Don't want to miss our deadline," said Roger, glancing uneasily left and right. "Get it—DEADline?"

T. J. shifted his shopping bag nervously.

"Come on, guys. Whatever we thought we saw or heard last time, it wasn't a ghost. There's no mystery that science can't explain. It's like when Sir Isaac Newton saw the apple fall from the tree and said, 'What goes up must come down.' Then he went on to figure out the laws of motion and gravity. He was the founder of modern science because of—"

"Okay, Great Brain, but I bet old Newton never went into a haunted house," said Roger.

"Maybe not, but he proved that everything in nature can be explained," I said.

I trained my light on the crumbling steps of the side porch and jumped over the missing one all the way to the top. T. J. came next, holding his flashlight out like a sword, and Roger was right behind him.

I took a deep breath and slowly turned the knob. After all the pushing we did last time, now the door creaked right open. Boy, was it dark in there.

"This way." I walked around the table, past the refrigerator, and through the swinging door into the dining room.

It was darker in there and our eyes had to blink to adjust, even with the flashlights. One sweep around the room and I found the door. We edged our way past the long wooden table. Suddenly, a light appeared right in front of us.

"Aaahhh!"

"An orb." T. J.'s breath was in my ear as he grabbed my arm so hard it hurt.

"Um . . . Hello . . . um . . . Your . . . um . . . Ghostly . . ."

I swept my light around again and the light ahead of us moved, too.

"Guys," I said. "That's not an orb. It's my flashlight being reflected in the mirror on top of that cabinet with the dishes."

All three of us exhaled as we walked past the cabinet and through the door into the hallway. This room was brighter, as the rising moon shone through the tall windows.

We looked up the stairs. Even though I knew the ghost was just an illusion, it was hard not to remember that shadow moving and the creepy tap-tapping that sounded an awful lot like a peg leg hitting wood.

I aimed my flashlight up and down the stairs. T. J. and Roger pointed theirs, too.

"See. Nothing here."

CLINK! PLINK! CLINK! PLINK!

"What's that?"

I pointed the beam of my flashlight up. There was nothing on the stairs. I aimed the light up higher. The chandelier crystals were moving ever so slightly in the wind.

"You know that paranormal activity is heightened during the full moon," said T. J. "On account of increased magnetism on the earth plane."

"Well, that was just the chandelier," I said. "Not some ghostly manifestation. So don't take out your thermometer, Teej. We already know there is a draft in here that makes the temperature rise and fall. Now let's go."

We moved across the hall to the two facing doors. The one on the left was closed, and the one on the right was open. I could have sworn both doors were closed the last time we were here.

OOMPH! T. J. fell. Roger and I whipped around, flashlights blazing.

"What happened?"

T. J. stood up, holding a dark rectangular object: Roger's camera. "Look, Rog. It's not even dead. That means it probably picked up some footage of the entity."

"Thank you, Teej!" said Roger, taking the camera with a big grin on his face.

"T. J., how many times do I have to tell you? There are no such things as ghosts or entities or orbs or streaks or whatever. We have to find the harpoon."

"Eenie, meenie, miney, moe." Roger pointed from the closed door to the open door. "Catch a tiger by the toe. If he hollers, let him go—"

"Come on, Rog," I said. "We'll be here all night."

There was no logical reason to be nervous, but my heart started beating fast as I moved toward the closed door. I wasn't afraid of the ghost, but I had this creepy feeling we were being watched. I remembered what Venus had said about the ghost hanging around because it was unhappy.

I turned the knob and walked into the room. There was a fireplace at one end and a bunch of furniture covered with old sheets. Dust lined the floor, thick as a carpet. Over the fireplace hung a big gold-framed painting of a whaling ship chasing a whale that had been harpooned.

"Wow!" I said, moving closer and pushing the cobwebs away. "Look at that ship!"

"Look at all that blood," said Roger. "That whale's a goner."

"Please don't talk about blood," said T. J., looking green in the light of our flashlights.

"Hey, check out this ship in a bottle," said Roger, shining his flashlight on a small table in the middle of the room. "Cool."

"Look at this," said T. J., moving over to a glass-fronted cabinet filled with scrimshaw, carvings on whalebone sailors made when they were bored at sea.

BEEP! BEEP!

It was 8:15 already. We had to hurry.

"Bingo!" said Roger, standing in front of a closet. "I think it's our lucky day—I mean night."

"You found a harpoon?"

Roger pulled something long, skinny, and pointy out of the closet.

"TA-DA!"

"That's a curtain rod, Sherlock," I said.

"There's lots more stuff in here," said Roger, walking deeper into the closet. "A croquet set, a trunk, a vacuum cleaner, something longish and skinnyish made of metal. Could it be a har—"

"Nope," said T. J., coming up behind him "It's got a reel, which means it's a fishing pole."

"Hey, there's a rusty anchor," said Roger. "And a type-writer and one of those old phones you dial and tons more stuff."

Admiral Royce sure wasn't a very good housekeeper. It would take a while to dig through everything.

I noticed another door in the wall opposite the fireplace. I hadn't seen it at first because it was flush with the paneling and it had a very small knob. I turned the knob, figuring the door led to another closet. It didn't.

I walked through it, and with a soft PHOOMPH! the door shut behind me. I shined my light around. This room was longer and *L*-shaped. I walked in farther. The door at the opposite end that led out to the hall was open. So I was in the room next door. For a brief second I wondered if I should tell Roger and T. J. where I was, but then my flash-light found bookcases on three walls and a fireplace on the fourth wall.

The study. Just the room I was looking for.

Sheet-covered furniture filled this room, too, and more nautical memorabilia. An old compass under glass. Another ship in a bottle. There were books stuffed onto every shelf of the bookcases. There was a giant map of the Arctic and another map of the South Seas.

All of a sudden, I spotted something long and cylindrical, made of metal, propped in a corner between the fireplace and the window. Something sharp and pointed jutted from the end.

A harpoon!

But as I got closer, I realized it wasn't a harpoon at all. It was an extremely long fireplace poker. Darn!

In my hurry to put it back, I knocked into the wall of books behind me. And a narrow door in the bookcase swung open.

WHOA! A secret passage.

I bet Hannibal Royce really was an abolitionist. I mean, what better place to hide runaway slaves than in a secret passage? Once the Fugitive Slave Act was passed in 1850, making it a crime for anyone to harbor runaway slaves, he would have had to be extra careful. I stepped in and trained my light around the tiny room. It was empty except for a flight of stairs leading down into the darkness.

CLICK!

The door behind me closed. I shined my light, looking for the knob so I could open it. There wasn't one. I pushed against the wall with my shoulder where the door had to be. It didn't budge.

I rammed into it again. Nothing.

And again. Nothing.

"Roger! T. J.!" I banged on the wall.

No answer.

"Guys! Help!"

This was no time to panic. I felt around for my pocketknife. Maybe I could pry open the door with the spoon or the scissors. I jammed my scissors into the wood where I thought the seams of the door should be. No luck. It was as if the door had disappeared. That meant one thing—I couldn't get out the way I got in.

I had two options: Plan A—I could keep banging and yelling and hope Roger and T. J. would hear me, or Plan B— I could go down the stairs and try to find another way out.

BEEP! BEEP!

It was 8:30. It looked like I had no choice. Plan B.

I shined my light onto layers of dust and cobwebs that covered the stairs leading down to the basement. The basement where the one-legged whaler took his victims after he stabbed them with his bloody harpoon.

I put one foot down. And then another. The steps were steep and narrow, but they held my weight. I went down another step and then another. So far, so good. I came to a turn in the stairs. There was a rustling sound. In the beam of my flashlight, I caught a glimpse of a long gray tail.

Just a mouse.

I turned the corner. There was another, longer flight that led to the basement. It seemed even darker down there. I gulped, but I kept going.

The air was cool and damp. Goose bumps crawled over my skin. I remembered what T. J. had said about cold spots and entities sucking the heat energy out of the atmosphere so they could manifest.

As I went down another step into that inky-black darkness, I felt the EMF meter in my pocket bump against my leg. I started talking to myself, like I do when I'm worrying about stuff and can't sleep.

"The electromagnetic spectrum is a continuum of electromagnetic waves organized according to wavelength and frequency."

I took another step.

"The longest wavelengths with the lowest frequencies are radio waves."

I went down another two steps.

"Next come microwaves."

Another step.

"After that is infrared light and visible light."

Another step. Halfway there.

"Next comes ultraviolet light."

Another step and another. Three more steps and I would be at the bottom.

"Finally, there are X-rays, and then the waves with the shortest wavelength and highest frequency are—"

OOMPH! I tripped and fell. Worse than that, a greeny-yellowy light appeared in the darkness.

SNAP! An orb!

Then a strange voice murmured two words: "Gamma rays!"

My hand holding the flashlight shook. My heart was pounding so hard, it felt as if it would pop right out of my chest. That was when my flashlight went out.

GAMMA RAYS

The strongest form of electromagnetic radiation (a type of energy), which can kill most life forms. Neutron stars, pulsars, and black holes are sources of gamma rays—so are supernova explosions and the decay of radio-active material in space. Gamma rays can only be blocked by dense materials like lead or concrete.

I was alone in the darkness with an entity that had sucked up all the charge from brand-new double-A batteries. According to T. J. and Dr. Ghost B. Gone, that meant one thing—the entity was going to manifest.

It was the ghost of the one-legged whaler . . . and it was coming for me!

GHOSTS WEAR GLASSES?!

The green-yellow light crept closer.

I tried to remember what Dr. Ghost B. Gone had said to do to get rid of an entity. Hold hands, that was it, and say it was time for the entity to leave and be free. I couldn't hold anybody's hand, so I clasped mine together around the flashlight.

"It's time for you to leave. . . ." The words came out in a squeaky rush.

"Yeeeeeessssss," said the voice. It seemed to echo in the silence.

WHOA! Maybe there really was something to Dr. Ghost B. Gone's wacky theories after all.

"You . . . um . . . need to go free," I said more firmly. "So . . . um . . . go."

"I know," said the voice.

All of a sudden, the light split into two. A white light floated just below the green-yellow light. OHMYGOSH! Was that supposed to happen? Wasn't the entity supposed to disappear with a POOF, not turn into two separate entities?

"Do you know the way out?" asked a voice that sounded almost the same as the first voice, except deeper.

A shiver ran down my spine as the two lights approached. The hairs on the back of my neck stood up. I felt as if my feet had frozen to the floor.

The seconds seemed like hours. I watched the lights come closer. The green-yellow one was like two oval empty eyes. What the heck?! It wasn't eyes. It was glasses.

The ghost was wearing glasses?!

Before I could figure out what the first entity was doing, the white light floated from my toes to my head so we were eye level. I saw the white light was held by a shadowy hand. The hand of the ghost of the one-legged whaler?! Did that mean the bloody harpoon was in the other hand and I was about to be run through?!

Wait a minute! My eyes focused on the hand, and I saw that it was connected to an arm. And on the arm were those rope bracelets that surfers wear. I didn't think ghosts had solid arms, let alone surfed.

"I didn't mean to scare you," said a familiar voice, the light shining so I could see the voice's owner.

"You're not a ghost! You're the archaeologist from the supermarket!" I said.

"And you're one of the recycling boys," he said. "My name is Wallace W. Willis. I'm not an archaeologist, although I do love archaeology. It was my minor in college. My field of study is American history."

"I'm Fish. I knew you weren't a ghost hunter."

Wallace Willis looked uncomfortable for a minute. "I've been searching for a way out since yesterday afternoon," he said, changing the subject. "Even with my night-vision goggles, I couldn't find one. I was sure glad I left them in my backpack from my last camping trip, though, since it's so dark down here."

That explained the greeny-yellow light and the ghostly glasses. But it didn't explain why Wallace Willis was here. The one-legged whaler's house was definitely not a campsite.

"Luckily I had enough snacks in my pack so I didn't starve. But I couldn't call anyone because my phone has no signal."

THUMP! THUMP! We both looked up.

"That's got to be my friends, Roger and T. J.," I said.

Wallace led the way up the stairs since he was still wearing his night-vision goggles. I used his phone as a light so I wouldn't trip.

"Good evening, Your Entity," I heard Roger say when we got to the top. "We've come to help you in whatever way we can. Give us a sign you're here."

I banged on the wall.

"I think it's a poltergeist," Roger said. "Poltergeists make all the noise, right?"

"Do you think it got Fish?" T. J. said.

"Let me ask," said Roger. "I think it likes me. Do you have Fish with you?"

"I see a light," said T. J. "Maybe it's an orb, not a poltergeist."

"Let us out!" I yelled, as Wallace and I both banged on the door.

"Oh, no! I think it's an elemental," said T. J. "Only an elemental has enough power to bang like that. Poor Fish!"

"Think he's a goner?" said Roger.

"It's not an elemental!" I yelled. "It's me!"

"Fish!!! Where are you?"

"In here."

"Are you okay?"

"Yes."

"What about the ghost?" said Roger. "Is it . . . with you?"

"Yes."

"Holy haunting!" said Roger.

"Quit talking and let us out. See the fireplace?"

"Yup!"

"Lean on the bookcase next to it."

"Fish, are you sure you're okay? Did the ghost maybe suck out your great brain along with the rest of your electromagnetic energy, because a bookcase is not a—"

PHOOMPH!

"AAAAHHHH!"

The secret bookcase door swung open. Roger knocked into us. He would have fallen if Wallace hadn't caught him.

"Say hello to the ghost," I said.

"What?!" said Roger and T. J., jumping back in surprise, their flashlights in our faces.

"Quit shining the light in my eyes," I said.

"We were looking for you for . . ." Roger's voice trailed

off when he got a look at Wallace. "I didn't know ghosts wore glasses."

"He's not really a ghost," I said.

"You're the ghost hunter from the supermarket," said T. J. "I told you so, Fish. What kind of entity do you think is haunting this house? Is it an elemental? We called 1-555-GOS-TBGN to ask Dr. Ghost B. Gone, but he didn't answer."

Wallace burst out laughing.

"What's so funny?" I said.

"Dr. Ghost B. Gone doesn't answer the phone," said Wallace.

"How do you—"

"I have a confession to make," said Wallace. "I'm not a ghost hunter, but I work for ghost hunters."

Then it hit me why he looked so uncomfortable. "You work for Dr. Ghost B. Gone?!"

Wallace nodded. "I'm not supposed to say anything about the show, because I signed a contract saying that I wouldn't. That's why I acted so strange."

"You know Dr. Ghost B. Gone?" T. J.'s eyes were round as Frisbees.

"Holy haunting!" said Roger.

"You're actually part of Dr. Ghost B. Gone's paranormal investigating team?" T. J. went on. "That's why you're here? To find out if the house is really haunted? Wow!"

"Actually, I'm not here for Dr. Ghost B. Gone. I work for him to pay for graduate school by researching the history of old houses that people say are haunted. I don't do any paranormal investigating. Sometimes I get him coffee."

"Half-caff mocha latte with soy milk and three sugars," said T. J. Like I said, he watches that show way too much.

"So, why are you here, then?" I asked.

"Well, for two reasons," Wallace said. "One, because when I was researching the history of American whaling for my dissertation—that's this big paper you have to write to get your PhD—I came across some information about Hannibal Royce that made me think I might be related to him. Which leads me to reason two."

He reached into his backpack and pulled out a plastic folder. He opened it and carefully took out a crumbling piece of yellowed paper. He shined the light from his phone on it so we could see.

It was an advertisement from an old newspaper that read:

WHALEMAN'S SHIPPING LIST

Patent Rocket Harpoons and Guns fasten to and kill instantly whales of every species. With proper lines and boats such as were used by the officers of the Superior in 1860. Two months' notice required to fill an order for the season of 1862. Contact Hannibal W. Royce, Captain of the Superior.

Below that was a picture of a boat with a guy standing in it, shooting a harpoon at a whale. So Hannibal Royce really was an inventor, just like the Captain said.

"This piece of paper is all I know about my father's family, since he died before I was born. It was in an envelope that read 'Wallace W. Willis, Sr.—family tree.'"

"So, the one-legged whaler—I mean Hannibal Royce— was your great-great-great-great-I-don't-know-how-many-greats-grandfather, or something?"

Wallace shrugged. "I don't know. Maybe he was an uncle or a distant cousin. I know I'm not related to Admiral Royce. I looked up his family tree. It's a real mystery."

"Wow!" I said, the dare forgotten as I realized what this meant. "If you are the heir, the house won't get knocked down."

"I was planning to go to the local library today to find out more about a Frenchwoman named Matilda who might have been Hannibal Royce's first wife. If she was married to Hannibal Royce and they had a son or daughter, that's who I think I might be descended from. All I know is that she was from a small town in France called Bayonne. It's where the bayonet was invented. Anyway, it's the same town my dad's family was from. I never made it to the library, though. I've been stuck here since yesterday afternoon."

"See, I told you there was no ghost."

ROCKET HARPOON

One of the first was patented in 1861 by Thomas Welcome Roys, a whaler in Southampton, New York. A pipe over the shoulder fired a harpoon head attached to a rope and a high-explosive grenade into the whale. It had a better chance of staying in the whale than a harpoon thrown by hand because whales pulled boats with so much force, they often got away.

"I went into the study and happened upon the same door Fish did. I thought I heard a noise, so I stepped inside and the next thing I knew, I was locked in. Thanks for letting me out. I'm just glad I got to see this place, even if I'll never know what the connection is between my father and Hannibal Royce."

Wallace looked sad for a moment. I figured he was missing his dad. I tried to imagine what it would be like to never know your father and one whole side of your family. I couldn't. Wallace had to find out if he was related to Hannibal Royce. If he was, it would almost be like finding his father.

"The library's open tomorrow, you know," I said. "There's this great librarian called Ms. Valen, who—"

Wallace held up his hand. "I wish I could, but I have to get back to school. Remember that big paper I told you about? Well, I have to defend it this week. That means I have to answer lots of questions from some big-deal American history professors who will decide if I get my PhD or not."

"Snap!" said Roger. "The real estate king is going to buy the house when it goes out of probate on Friday. That's less than a week away. You've got to get the proof before then, or—"

"I know! We'll find out for you," I said. "We'll go to the library and do the research."

Wallace smiled. "Thanks a lot, guys. Here's my cell phone number. Let me know what you turn up. But don't worry if you don't find anything. I think it's a real long shot."

BEEP! BEEP!

"Guys, it's eight-forty-five," I said. "We've got to get going."

"But we don't have the harpoon," said Roger. "You didn't happen to see a harpoon down there, did you?"

Wallace shook his head. We explained about the dare and the crowd of kids outside. He agreed to wait till we left before he went on his way. He wanted to spend a little more time in the house anyway.

"We'll let you know as soon as we find anything out," I said.

"Say hello to Dr. Ghost B. Gone from me," said T. J. "Tell him I'm his number-one fan!"

"Oh, brother," I said.

My mind was spinning with thoughts about Wallace, the one-legged whaler, and how we could save the house. The dare wasn't the last thing on my mind, but it wasn't the first when we got to the end of the driveway. There were fewer kids than before, but Mi and Si were still there. They whooped when they saw us. Bryce was sitting on his scooter. The bright yellow gleamed in the silvery moonlight.

"Fish!" Clementine ran up to me. "You're okay?" She leaned over like she was about to hug me and then stepped back quickly.

"Hi, Clementine. I'm—"

"So, where's the harpoon, losers?" said Bryce.

T. J., Roger, and I exchanged glances.

"Looks like I win," said Bryce with a nasty grin.

"No, you don't," I said.

Roger raised one eyebrow. T. J. looked at me in surprise.

"We didn't find the harpoon," I said. "Because we were too busy finding something way more important."

All eyes were on me as the crowd moved closer. Bryce sneered. "Like what?"

"The heir, that's what."

"No way!" said Trippy and True, but they sure looked surprised.

"What?!" said Bryce as the kids crowded even closer.

"We met someone we're pretty sure is the heir," I said. "And we're going to . . ."

"What? Where is he? You're lying, Finelli."

Trippy and True shook their heads.

"He's in the one-legged whaler's house right now," I said. "His name is Wallace, and—"

"There's no heir," said Bryce. "People who know how to find heirs looked and they didn't find one. You're telling me you just did?! No way."

"Go inside and see if you don't believe me."

Bryce's eyes darted to the overgrown trees and the old house looming darkly through them. "Even if you did meet someone who said he's the heir, he's not."

"How do you know?"

"Because my dad is buying that house no matter what you say, loser!"

"Oh, yeah?!"

Bryce rolled his eyes. "Whatever, Dork Breath. You didn't get the harpoon, so you lose—which means I win."

Roger and T. J. looked at me. I looked at Bryce, my face getting hot, the way it does when I start to get mad. I was about to start yelling about how we weren't losers and we would *so* find the harpoon, but then I thought about Wallace and how sad he was about his dad and his family. I thought about my mom and Venus talking about how the house was a special landmark in our town.

"You know what, Bryce? I don't care. A harpoon is nowhere near as important as an heir. We're going to prove Wallace is the rightful heir, and then your dad won't be able to buy the one-legged whaler's house and destroy it."

"You'll never prove it, loser," said Bryce.

"Oh yes, we will. . . ."

Roger and T. J. looked at me, their eyes wide. No one had found proof of Hannibal Royce having another family, not even historians and librarians and the experts who research inheritance laws.

"No one beats my dad," Bryce said, turning on his cool yellow scooter and revving the engine. "He always wins!"

"Not this time!" I yelled over the sound. "Just you wait and see. . . ."

THE SECRET OF THE STINKY SOCK

"April Day! April Day!"

I knew that little voice. Feenie sounded scared. I had to help her. I tried to move, but my arms and legs were bound by firm ropes. All of a sudden, a green and yellow light appeared. An orb! And it was heading down the long dark tunnel—right for Feenie.

"Look out for the ghost, Feenie!"

"It's not a ghost, silly, it's a fairy," Feenie said. Then she sneezed: AH-CHOO!

I woke up with a start. I wasn't in a long, dark tunnel. I was in my sleeping bag on the floor of Roger's basement.

I wiggled my head out so I could breathe. *What a strange dream.* It reminded me of Feenie's nonsense message from the Captain. Only now I realized it wasn't nonsense.

"Rog! Rog! Wake up!"

I nudged Roger, who was sleeping next to me.

"Ugh . . . can't you see I'm sleeping?"

"If you're talking, then you're not sleeping."

"I'm sleep talking."

"Listen. Remember the two hundred raisins on a hill and the—"

"I hate word problems when I get them for homework during school, so why would I want to solve one just for fun during summer vacation?"

"It's not a word problem," I said, sitting up. "It's a message. Feenie said the Captain said AH-CHOO. I thought that meant he sneezed. I think what he really said was SNAFU, which sounds like AH-CHOO."

"Oooooookkkkaaaaaayyyyy," yawned Roger. "What's SNAFU again?"

"Situation Normal All Fouled Up. It's Navy slang for a big problem. So then he said two hundred raisins on a hill, which was really an address."

"I still don't get it," said Roger.

"It means he was letting me know there was a problem at the one-legged whaler's house, which is at 200 Raven Hill . . ."

". . . which sounds like raisins on a hill," Roger said. "Wow! Good duct-tape reasoning, Oh, Great Brainio."

"Deductive reasoning, not duct-tape reasoning," I said.

"I know," said Roger. "Where's your sense of humor? Did you leave it back on Raisin Hill? Now can I go back to sleep?"

"How can you sleep at a time like this?"

"It's seven o'clock on Sunday morning, when all normal people sleep."

"Do I smell pancakes?" T. J. said from the other side of Roger.

"Nah, it's just the tangy aroma of the Great Brain's brains frying themselves from thinking so hard," said Roger.

"Oh," said T. J. Then he fell back to sleep on top of the empty bag of cookies we'd eaten last night.

"Wake up, Teej!" I started pacing. "You too, Roger." I poked him with my toe. "We have to go see the Captain. He must know something important about the one-legged whaler's house that he wants to tell me. He probably said Mayday, which is a distress signal, since time is running out. Feenie said April, but she meant May. She gets the months mixed up. She still thinks there's a month between June and July called Julune."

Roger faked loud snoring sounds.

"The Captain would only say Mayday if something was really wrong and it was really important. Come on, guys. Let's go."

"It's too early," said Roger. "The Captain will be sleeping."

"No, he won't. He always gets up at five o'clock. He had the dawn watch in the Navy."

T. J. and Roger burrowed back into their sleeping bags, so I had no choice. I grabbed the pillows off the couch and started throwing them.

"Pillow fight!" yelled Roger, lobbing his pillow at me.

I ducked and it hit T. J., who sat up so fast I tripped over him, knocked into Roger, and landed on an unopened bag of seaweed crisps, the snack option provided by Mrs. H.

The bag exploded. Seaweed crisps popped out all over the floor.

MAYDAY

Emergency code word used as a distress signal in radio communications. Comes from French m'aidez (meaning "help me"), which sounds like "mayday" in English. It is always given three times in a row: Mayday Mayday Mayday. It was started by a London airport radio officer in 1923.

They smelled salty and fishy, kind of like Uncle Norman's tackle box. "Hmm," said T. J., eating one. "Not bad."

After we cleaned up Roger's basement, we hopped on our bikes and headed down my driveway.

"So, Great Brain, how exactly are we going to prove Wallace is the heir?" said Roger. "By finding some secret documents no one ever found before, that not even Ms. Valen knows about?"

"Um . . . yeah . . . something like that," I said. In the light of day, it was kind of a crazy idea, but we had to do it. We had to prove Wallace was the heir. Some way. Somehow.

Like my dad always says, what's right is right. And this was right. We had to save the one-legged whaler's house. I had a feeling that was exactly what the Captain wanted me to do. Hopefully he had something that would help.

It was a hot, steamy morning, and I was sweating by the time we got to Red Fox Lane. T. J. ran in to tell his mom we were going to the Captain's. When he came out, he was chomping on another big wad of gum. He blew a bubble. It was orange and green and smelled like a pot of my mom's gravy with lots of oregano and tomatoes. Weird.

"I feel like I'm eating a slice at Tony's," said Roger.

"That's because it's pizza-flavored gum," said T. J. as we turned toward Whale Rock and pulled up to the Captain's house.

There was a car parked in the driveway beside the old rusty Range Rover the Captain drives. It was a silver hatchback with Texas license plates. It had a bumper sticker that read NURSES MAKE IT ALL BETTER!

"Go home, y'all!" called a woman's voice with a twangy accent.

"Hi, Ms. Worth," I said, walking toward the front door, where the Captain's daughter was standing with her hands on her hips. She was wearing a pair of hot pink scrubs and her bright red hair was piled up on top of her head. "It's me, Fish. We came to see the Captain, and—"

"Oh, no, you don't!" she said. "Don't any of y'all come one step closer!"

"Ms. Worth, we just want to talk to—"

"I said not a step closer, and I meant it!" She shook a finger at me.

"But why?" I said. "I know the Captain would like to see me, ma'am."

"The Captain isn't seein' anybody right now. He has contracted walking pneumonia."

"I didn't know you could get sick from walking," said T. J.

"It's not from walking," said the Captain's daughter. "It's called that because you don't know you have it, so you walk around as if you're well when you one hundred percent are not. My father will dig himself into an early grave if he doesn't listen to me."

Roger and T. J. looked at me and shrugged.

"Now, you three scoot so you don't catch it."

"We didn't bring a net, so we can't catch it," said Roger.

"Funny boy. Listen here, the Captain needs his rest. So off you go." Ms. Worth closed the front door with a bang.

"Now what are we going to do?"

A red flare suddenly streaked over our heads. The Captain, wearing a bathrobe, his blue-and-gold captain's hat, and a pair of black knee socks, was standing on the widow's walk on top of the house. He was waving his arms wildly and pointing to the backyard.

"Let's go!" I said.

The three of us biked across the grass to the back of the house.

"Admiral Royce left this clue!" The Captain called down to us, waving a piece of yellowed paper in the air. He was a little pale, but besides that he looked okay. That walking pneumonia sure was a sneaky illness. "It tells where to find Hannibal Royce's whaling log and diary."

"Why did he hide a—"

"It's a search-and-recovery mission, men. The admiral was a secretive old chap and he was convinced that someone might steal what he had come to believe was proof that there was another branch of the Royce family. I didn't realize I had this until a few days ago. It was mixed up with other papers he gave me. Plus, at the time, I must admit I didn't know whether to believe him, because he was a little, shall we say, crazy, on the subject. . . . Anyway, move out on the double. Time is not on your side." Then he pointed to his eyes. "Eyes only."

"Where is this log?"

"In the study, where you usually find books," said the Captain.

"Captain, we think we might have found the heir," I said. "He had this rocket harpoon ad his father left him 'cause Hannibal Royce was in his family tree, and he—"

"Welcome?" asked the Captain.

"Thank you?" said Roger.

The Captain frowned down at us. "The *W* is for Welcome."

"The *T* is for thank you," Roger called back.

The Captain shook his head so hard, his captain's hat fell off. "Welcome is the name—"

"Peepaw, what are you doing up there?" Ms. Worth's voice was so loud, we could hear it all the way out in the backyard. "You come down this instant."

The Captain's eyes darted from us to the piece of paper.

"Peepaw, I mean it!"

SKKKRRRREAK! came the sound of a window being opened.

The Captain quickly bent and pulled off one of his socks. He folded the piece of paper and shoved it inside. Then he tossed the sock down to us.

"Get it, guys!" I said as we got set to catch the Captain's flying sock.

"Ace outfielder Fast-Hands Huckleton dives for the ball. And he's got it," said Roger. "The crowd goes—PEE-YEW!" He tossed the sock at me.

"I can smell it all the way over here," said T. J.

I held on to it with two fingers. The guys were right. The sock smelled like rotten eggs and leftover Brussels sprouts. The Captain must have really sweaty feet. He could sure use those Odor-Eaters pads my dad wears in his work boots.

The last thing I wanted was to stick my hand in there, but I couldn't wait to get a look at the mysterious clue Admiral Royce had left behind.

"Hurry up, Fish," said Roger, scrunching up his nose. "PEE-YEW! This waiting around sure stinks, if you know what I mean."

I pulled the clue out with one hand and held my nose with the other. Carefully, I unfolded the piece of paper. It was graph paper. On it the Admiral had drawn twelve rectangles of different colors. One was all white with a red square in the middle, one was half blue and half red, one was made up of four smaller yellow and black rectangles, and one was half red and half white. Others were different combinations of the same colors in triangular, square, and star shapes.

"Huh?" said Roger. "The secret of the stinky sock remains a secret to me. What kind of code is that?"

"It's like those paintings we saw that time we went on the field trip to the museum and Two O hurled on the bus 'cause he ate all those Red Hots," said T. J.

"Nasty," said Roger. "How could I forget, since I was his seat partner?"

"Guys, please," I said.

"Remember those paintings?" said T. J. "They were all different colors in different shapes. Some were even just drips of paint, like—"

"Oh, yeah," said Roger.

"Guys, come on. Let me think."

"There was that one of the American flag," Roger went on. "But the stars were just blobs of white paint and the stripes were all wiggly. It didn't look like any American flag I ever—"

"That's it! All those symbols look like flags."

"They don't look like the flags of any countries I know," said Roger.

"Those aren't country flags," I said. "I think they might be nautical flags. I mean, Admiral Royce was in the Navy, so it makes sense that he would use a nautical code. I remember reading about nautical signal flags in a book. I don't remember how you use them and if each flag is a letter or a word or what they represent exactly."

"So, how are we going to read the message?" said T. J.

"We need to do some research," I said.

"Research and summer vacation are two words that just do not go together," Roger sighed.

"That's three words," said T. J.

"Exactly," said Roger. "My brain is on vacation till September."

"Not anymore," I said. "Remember, we're going to the library tomorrow anyway. It's the perfect place to wake up your brain. . . ."

THAR SHE BLOWS!

We got to the library as soon as it opened. Roger wanted to look up nautical flags on the internet, but I headed straight for the encyclopedias. In the *MNO* volume, I found what I was looking for.

"Guys! Come here!"

T. J. and Roger were huddled over a computer across the room.

"I'm telling you, *nautical* is spelled *n-a-w-t-i-k-a-l*," T. J. said. "Remember phonics?"

"You mean, remember inventive spelling?" said Roger. "The real way to spell it is *n-a-u-h-t*—you know how they slide in those silent letters just to confuse us on spelling tests."

"Guys, I got it."

Roger and T. J. hurried over. "Look! I was right. It's an international nautical signal code. Each flag corresponds to a letter. There are twenty-six flags for the twenty-six letters of the alphabet. So that red-, white-, and blue-striped one is *T*. And the red-and-white one is *H*."

"The sixth flag is the same, so that's another *H*," said T. J.

"Woo-hoo! Wonder what it says?" Roger hopped up and down.

I pulled out my notebook and pen and started writing down the letter for each of the nautical signal flags in the Admiral's message.

"Hurry up, Fish!" said Roger.

"I'm hurrying," I said, writing down the last two letters.

T-H-A-R-S-H-E-B-L-O-W-S

"Thar she blows," said Roger.

"I feel like I've heard that

INTERNATIONAL SIGNALING FLAGS

Used to signal between two ships or ship and shore, they include 26 square flags, one for each letter of the alphabet. Since only some colors in some combinations can be seen at sea, they are designed in red and white, yellow and blue, blue and white, and black and white, or plain red, white, or blue.

before," said T. J., blowing a purple bubble with his gum. The smell of Banana Berry Blast bubble gum filled the air.

"Teej, no blowing bubbles in the library," I hissed, making sure no librarian had spotted us.

POP!

"Thar she blows!" said Roger, nudging T. J., whose bubble had popped all over his face.

"Guys, will you be serious? We need to figure out this clue. 'Thar she blows' is what sailors used to say when they spotted a whale as water was shooting out of its blowhole. I don't understand how that will lead us to the whaling log's hiding place."

"Maybe it's the name of a book," said T. J. "Since the Captain said it was in the study."

"But the whaling log *is* a book, so how can a book be in a book?" I closed my notebook. "Let's go see Ms. Valen and start our research on Hannibal Royce. Maybe the research will give us a clue."

I led the way down a long wood-paneled corridor to the door with the gold writing that read SPECIAL COLLECTION. BY APPOINTMENT ONLY. We knocked, since we didn't have an appointment.

"How can I help you boys today?" Ms. Valen said, opening the door for us to come in.

"We're looking for information about Hannibal Royce," I said.

Ms. Valen smiled. "Thinking about the mysterious gravestone old Mrs. Osborn mentioned and the long-lost heir?"

"We found a secret pass—" began T. J.

"You never know what secrets you might find when you do research," I said, glaring at T. J. We couldn't tell Ms. Valen about the secret passage, because then we'd have to tell her we had snuck into the house and snooped around.

"There isn't much information," she said, pointing to a shelf where there was one fat brown leather-bound book and two much thinner black ones. "Nineteenth-century records were not kept very well. And we don't have any of his whaling logs or ship diaries. Those are very useful because captains, like Hannibal Royce, wrote in them about everything that happened on board ship, including what the crew ate, whale sightings, and the weather. They often jotted down their own personal thoughts, too."

She put the books on the table along with three pairs of white cotton gloves. "Put these on first."

"To check for dust, like those commercials on TV where the lady runs her finger over the furniture to make sure it's clean?" said T. J.

"No, it's to keep the oil in your skin from getting onto the pages. Oil can damage the paper because it's so old." Ms. Valen pointed to the thin black books. "One is the birth records for Whooping Hollow from 1700 till 1850, and the other is the death records, which is really a catalog of cemetery headstones from that period."

We put on our gloves. "Teej, you take the birth records. Rog, you take the cemetery headstones."

I started reading the fat book, *Nineteenth-Century Whaling Masters*. There was a whole section on Hannibal Royce that said pretty much what we already knew. It also said something about how he met a woman named Matilda St. Clair on a whaling trip in 1846, when his ship stopped in France. It was rumored she returned home with him and became his first wife, dying shortly afterward, though there is no record of the marriage. . . . That must be the same woman Wallace had mentioned.

"Hey, Ms. Valen, it says right here Hannibal may have had a first wife," I said. "The Frenchwoman."

"I know, but there is no proof that he did. And that book states clearly that it was a rumor," said Ms. Valen.

I returned to my reading. Hannibal Royce was officially married in 1855 to a woman named Mary Hand. They had one son named Philander. He had to be the ancestor of Admiral Thomas Royce, since according to the book, Hannibal Royce didn't have any more wives or any more kids.

"Teej, look up the year 1855 and see if a kid named Philander Royce was born."

"That's a weird name," said T. J., paging through the book. "No Philander in 1855."

"How about 1856?"

T. J. shook his head.

"Keep looking. Now, Roger, see if someone named Matilda St. Clair Royce died in 1847 or 1848."

"Who was that again?"

"The one who might have been Hannibal's first wife."

"I got it!" said T. J. all of a sudden. "Philander Royce was born on August 21, 1857."

"Good job, Teej. Finally, we're getting somewhere. Hey, was there another Royce kid born earlier, in like 1846 or 1847?"

"Hey, how weird is this?" said Roger. "'Stranger, stop and cast an eye. As you are now, so once was I. As I am now, so you will be. Remember Death and follow me. Philander Royce 1775 to 1830.'"

"I bet that was Hannibal Royce's dad, and then Hannibal named his kid after him," I said.

Ms. Valen nodded. "Although the inscription is a bit creepy, it was very popular on tombstones in the late eighteenth century."

"No Matilda Royce," said Roger. "Just Hannibal Welcome Royce, Whaling Captain, Killer of monsters of the deep, 1816 to 1886."

"Welcome," I said. "Hmm . . ." Why did that name sound so familiar, and why did it seem important?

"Then 'Philander Royce, Husband and Father. In the arms of angels 1857 to 1901.'"

"That Philander Royce was Admiral Thomas Royce's great-grandfather," said Ms. Valen.

I went back to the book to see if there was anything else about the Frenchwoman, Matilda, but the next part of the book was all about how Hannibal Royce was the first American whaler to hunt for whales in the Arctic and how he patented a bunch of whaling inventions, like the rocket harpoon. There was even a picture of an advertisement like the one Wallace had shown us. Interesting, but not exactly helpful in terms of finding out more about whether he had a first wife.

I kept reading just in case there was something.

"Oh, man! You'll never believe this!" I said.

"What?" said Roger, as he, T. J., and Ms. Valen looked over at me.

"You know how Hannibal Royce lost his leg?"

"Yeah, a great white or some big old whale bit it—" began Roger.

I shook my head. "He blew it off when he was testing out the rocket harpoon he invented. And he was all the way out in the Arctic whale hunting when it happened, so then he had to stay in some hospital there to recover."

"Whoa!" said Roger and T. J. as I scanned the rest of the page.

"The doctor said he thought Hannibal would die 'cause his leg got infected. But Hannibal Royce said he couldn't die because he had a wife with a child on the way and he had to get home to them." I looked up, my eyes wide. "You know what this means?"

"He was one tough dude," said Roger.

"Totally, but it also means that he had a family when this accident happened, so if it happened before he married Mary Hand, then it means—"

"He married the Frenchwoman what's-her-name?"

"Matilda St. Clair," I said.

"Well, when was the accident?"

I read each page three times, but I couldn't find a date for the accident or for the voyage.

"Thanks, Ms. Valen," I said, taking off my gloves. "If only we could track down some proof that Matilda St. Clair married Hannibal Royce and then find out if they had a kid."

Ms. Valen sighed. "I know. But there is no proof she even existed, let alone married him and had a child and then died. With only a few more days until the house is out of probate, it looks as if it will be torn down."

We had to find that whaling log and ship's diary. It was the only way to stop Benedict Billings. And we'd have to hurry. We were running out of time. . . .

BOOzarre BUT TRUE!

"I just know the whaling log will prove that Wallace is the heir. We have to find it," I said as we headed out to Raven Hill Road.

"Gum?" said T. J., handing Roger a piece when we stopped at the stop sign on Main Street.

"Thanks," said Roger. "Plain old bubble gum, my favorite."

"You're welcome," said T. J.

"Welcome!" I repeated excitedly as an idea formed in my mind. "I bet Welcome is Wallace's middle name. I just remembered he said his name was Wallace W. Willis. I bet the *W* stands for Welcome, just like Hannibal Welcome Royce. And that's why the Captain—"

"Kept saying *welcome* when I said *thank you*," said Roger.

"Because he thought the heir was named Welcome, too. I have to call Wallace and ask him. If it is his name, there is no way that is just a coincidence."

We were halfway down Main Street when we noticed some kids coming out of Get Whooped.

"So, where's the *heir, air*heads?" said Bryce, shifting his brand-new skateboard from one hand to the other. It was one of the real expensive hand-designed ones with top-of-the-line trucks and wheels.

"I bet nobody was even in the house in the first place," said Trippy.

"Yeah," agreed True, flipping up his board and catching it in one hand. "You just said that 'cause you didn't find the harpoon."

The three of them blocked the sidewalk, so it was either run them over or stop. We stopped. That's when I noticed Clementine standing off to the side. She must have just come out of the store, too. She had a Get Whooped bag in her hand with a pair of swimming goggles poking out of the top.

"I believe you, Fish," she said.

"I don't," said Bryce, rolling his eyes. "Loser."

"It's so strange that you met the heir that very night," Clementine went on.

"BOOzarre but true," agreed Roger.

"It wasn't an accident," said T. J. "The ghost made sure it happened, so we can help him."

"Help him do what?" asked Trippy even though Bryce was shooting daggers at him with his eyes.

"Help him keep the house in his family and keep it from being destroyed."

Bryce shook his head. "Well, tough luck to the ghost. My dad's going to be knocking that house down next week."

"No, he's not," I said. "We're on our way there right now to get the final proof."

"Just like you got the harpoon, huh, loser?" sneered Bryce.

"You'll see," I said, my ears starting to burn. I tried not to think about how even the Captain had thought Admiral Royce was a little crazy when it came to the Royce family tree.

"No, you'll see, Dork Breath," said Bryce. "Nobody stops my dad."

"Yeah," said Trippy, and True nodded.

"Well, maybe this time somebody will," I said, fingering Admiral Royce's clue in my pocket.

"Yeah, right. As if you have the power to do anything. You're just a kid. And your dad's nobody. He's just a plumber," said Bryce.

"How dare you—" I began as Clementine mouthed something to me that I suddenly realized was the word *jealous*. Bryce, Trippy, and True didn't hear me, because they were already walking away.

"Good luck, Fish!" Clementine called before heading after them.

"He makes me so mad," I said as the three of us pedaled toward Raven Hill. My whole face was burning just thinking about big-mouth Bryce. What did it matter if being jealous only made him mean? "We have to find that log. We'll show him and his dad and—"

"Whoa there, Great Brain! You know you have more brain power in your little finger than Bryce has in his entire big head."

T. J. laughed, and then I did, too.

"At least we know we've got nothing to be scared of," said Roger as we headed up the long driveway. "Since there is no ghost."

"I wouldn't be so sure," said T. J. "Entities only show themselves when they want to, you know."

"Teej, please. What we need to do now is plain old investigating—not the paranormal kind—and find a real, live book left behind by a real, live person.

"We already know there's no such thing as ghosts," I said as we slipped through the side door into the kitchen and headed across the hallway. "Remember, it was just Wallace."

"Maybe. Maybe not."

In the afternoon light, the place looked less spooky and much more dusty than the last time we were there. It felt different, too—more welcoming, somehow. We headed into the library, and I pulled out the Admiral's clue.

"Thar she blows!" said Roger, heading over to a small painting of a whale breaching—you know, jumping out of the water—that was similar to the one in the living room, but without the harpoon and all the blood.

"Thar she blows!" T. J. picked up a piece of scrimshaw with a whale design carved onto it.

"Thar she blows!" I said, studying a section of one bookcase in the three walls of bookcases around the room. This one was filled with books about whales and whaling.

I pulled out one titled *Monsters of the Deep*. There was nothing hidden behind it, so I started flipping through the dusty pages.

The next bookcase had more books about whaling voyages and marine science mixed up with books about whaling ships and navigation. The books weren't arranged in any order that I could tell and seemed to be shoved in every which way.

"Hey, guys, come here," said Roger. "I need some help." He had climbed on top of the cabinet next to the painting. "You pull that side and I'll pull this side."

"You think there's a safe hidden behind the painting with the whaling log inside it?" I said.

"Great minds think alike," said Roger as we pulled the dusty old painting off the wall. No luck. There was just a large white rectangle where the painting had been.

"Drat!" said Roger. "That's always where people hide stuff in the movies."

"These are made of whalebone, right?" T. J. picked up a piece of scrimshaw. "Maybe one of them will—"

"Trigger a secret compartment," said Roger. "Brilliant, Teej!" He picked up more pieces of scrimshaw. Nothing happened.

"I'm telling you, it's a book about a whale and the log is probably hidden—"

"Great Brain," said Roger, "these books are all about whales. *Whales of the Eastern Seaboard. Whale Oil Lights Up a Century.*" All of a sudden he grinned. "How will we ever find the right whale? Get it? You said the one-legged whaler was the first to catch right whales, right?"

"Then we'll have to pull out each one," I said. "Unless the title of one of them is *Thar She Blows!*"

Roger sighed as we stared at the rows and rows of books.

"Hey, see that fat one at the top with the gold letters?" said T. J. "It's called *Moby-Dick.* They were always saying, 'Thar she blows!' in the movie. I've seen it a bunch of times 'cause it's my dad's favorite. I knew it sounded familiar. It's about this crazy captain whose leg got bitten off by this whale."

"Another one-legged whaler," said Roger. "BOOzarre."

"I don't know, Teej," I said, pulling out a big book on sperm whales. There was nothing hidden inside it, and no whaling log in its spot in the bookcase.

"I just have a feeling," said T. J.

"This isn't about feelings," I said, pulling out the next book in the row. This one was about whaling ship design.

MOBY-DICK

A novel published in 1851 by Herman Melville about a great white whale, Moby-Dick, and the whaling captain who hunted him. It is based on Melville's own experiences on whaling ships and the real-life sinking of a famous whale ship, the *Essex*, which was attacked and sunk by a sperm whale.

"This is about facts. We have to do this the scientific way, pulling out each book. It's the process of elimination."

"Call it what you want; it'll take forever," said Roger. "Teej might be right. It sure beats going through a gazillion books. You said yourself we're running out of time." He climbed onto the fireplace and reached up to the top shelf.

"Heads up!" said Roger. He tossed a big book down. I almost dropped it because it was so heavy.

"I'm telling you, the only way to do this is to pull out each book and examine it," I said as I opened the cover. T. J. crowded closer.

"Nothing up here," said Roger.

"Nothing in here," I said, flipping the book open.

"Let me see," said T. J., reaching for it at the same moment that I moved forward to put it on the mantel.

PHWOMP! We collided. The book fell open with a thud. A small book fell out. It had been hidden in a hole that had been carved in the very center of the big book.

WHOA!

"Thar she blows!" said Roger.

I bent down and picked up the little book and turned to the first page:

The Log Book of the Ship Superior *and Diary of Captain Hannibal W. Royce, Master, Sailed on the 25th Day of June, 1847.*

We all stared at it in awe. It was the one-legged whaler's logbook and diary!

"How did you know?" I asked T. J.

He looked at me, his blue eyes serious. "The ghost told me. . . ."

CREAK! CREAK! TAP! TAP!

"What was that?" said Roger.

"It's the entity," said T. J. "I told you."

WHOOSH! TAP! TAP! CLINK!

My heart beat faster as T. J., Roger, and I exchanged glances. I was sure there was no ghost, but still. Something was making those sounds.

"Maybe it's a mouse or a rat," I said.

CLINK! CLINK! TAP! TAP!

"That sounds like the chandelier," said Roger. "Maybe the ghost is—"

Suddenly, we heard the murmur of voices and the thudding of what had to be footsteps coming closer.

"That's no ghost," I said.

"If it's not a ghost, then who could it be?" said Roger.

"I bet it's Bryce and those guys trying to scare us," I said. "They're the only ones who know we're here."

"Let's hide," said Roger. "We'll give them the fright of their lives."

"I don't know if that's such a good idea," said T. J.

The footsteps were just outside the door.

"Quick! We have to hide."

The door was opening.

"In here," I said, putting the book in my pocket as I knocked into the bookcase next to the mantel. It swung open.

We slipped inside the secret passage. This time I made sure to leave it open a crack.

"When I give the signal, we'll jump out," I whispered.

We huddled together by the crack in the door, trying to see out.

"What a beautiful room," said a woman's voice that sounded oddly familiar and nothing like Bryce, Trippy, or True. "Those are the original crenellated moldings. Seems such a pity to destroy history."

"No way!" Roger said.

"Shh!" I nudged him.

"It's a lot of old junk," said a man's deep voice as the two figures walked into our view.

They definitely were not Bryce and his buddies. They were none other than Benedict Billings and Mrs. H., Roger's mom. She worked for him part-time as a real estate agent.

"Don't you think you're getting a little ahead of yourself?" said Mrs. H. "I mean, the house doesn't officially go out of probate for a few more days."

She walked right up to the bookcase. She was inches from our faces. Roger sucked in his breath.

"Did you hear something?" said Mrs. H.

"I'm telling you, this place is mine. It's not like an heir is going to suddenly pop out of the woodwork," Mr. Billings said, coming over to stand behind her and knocking on the shelf right where we were standing.

We jumped back just as the tiny crack closed and the bookcase swung to with a click.

We were locked in the secret passage.

"Oh, jeepo!" said T. J.

"You can say that again," said Roger. "Now what? If my mom catches us, we're dead."

"If they don't let us out, then we're stuck in here," I said. "Like Wallace."

"With the ghost," added T. J., with a shiver.

We started banging, but it was no use. Mrs. H and Benedict Billings were already gone.

"What are we going to do?" said Roger.

I pulled out my flashlight and turned it on, lighting up the dusty, cobwebby stairs. Then the three of us headed slowly down to the basement.

Just because Wallace hadn't found a way out didn't mean there wasn't one. Either way, what other choice did we have?

At least it wasn't as dark as last time. Dusty gray streaks of light slanted in through two small windows at the far end of the room. Roger followed my gaze.

"You got a shrinking potion in your pocket?" he said. "'Cause there's no way we can fit through there."

"Let's see," I said, heading over to the window. "Help me move the boxes out of the way so you can climb up."

"Me?" said Roger.

"Yeah, you're the skinniest," I said. "If anybody's going to fit through that window, it's you."

We started moving boxes around. After a few minutes of helping, T. J. sat down on an armchair that had lost one of its arms in the corner next to the window. It was beside a big old-fashioned cupboard that had lots of dusty, cobwebby stuff on its shelves.

"Come on, Teej," I said. "Help us."

"Snap!" Roger exclaimed, staring at the cupboard. "I don't believe it."

"What?"

"Darth Billings has been beaten once more."

"Huh?"

"Right there, just above T. J.'s head. Look!"

I followed his finger. He was pointing at one of the dusty shelves. T. J. reached up and pulled down a long black pole spotted with rust with a point on the end.

"The harpoon!"

WOO-HOO!

After we finished whooping, I said, "That's great, but we still need to find a way out. So get over here, Teej!"

"I'm running out of energy," he said, propping the harpoon against the wall. "You guys want a piece of lemon gum?"

Roger and I shifted another box. He could climb up now, but the window really was pretty small. Hmm. Maybe if he took off his big baggy shorts, he could fit.

"Darn!" said T. J. "I dropped the pack."

"T. J., how can you think about gum at a time like this?" I said. "We need to find a way out before—"

"Whoa!"

"Teej, c'mon," I said.

"G-uh-ys," said T. J.

Roger and I looked around. "What?"

T. J. was on his hands and knees on the floor, his head under the cupboard. He slid back out, cobwebs sticking all over him. "There's a door in the floor."

WHAT???!!!

Roger jumped down. It took all three of us to move the cupboard. T. J. was right. Underneath was a door. A trapdoor, like the kind that leads up to the attic in my house.

It was fastened with two rusty iron bolts. I pulled on them as hard as I could, but they were pretty jammed. I pushed and pulled some more, and so did Roger and T. J. Finally, the bolts slid back.

We looked at one another. My heart started beating faster. Who knew what we were going to find beyond that door?

"Do you think there are skeletons in there?" whispered T. J. "Old bones from the bodies that got run through by the bloody harpoon?"

Roger's eyes went wide. "Maybe we should . . . wait . . . for . . ."

"This could be our only way out," I said, trying to sound braver than I felt. I wasn't afraid of ghosts, but I kept thinking about rats and giant spiders and other slimy creatures that like dark places.

"Fish is right," said T. J. as Roger nodded.

"Here goes nothing." I pulled on the door.

It wouldn't budge.

"Come on, guys, help me."

"Hey, I know." T. J. brought over the harpoon.

"Good idea, Teej," I said. "Leverage."

I slipped the point of the harpoon under the handle. Then I pushed down on the metal pole. No go. Roger put his hands over mine and T. J. put his hands over Roger's.

"On the count of three," I said. "One . . . two . . . three!"

We all pushed on the harpoon as hard as we could.

SKKRREEEEEAAAKKKK! The door flew open.

THWOMP! The three of us fell backward as a great cloud of dust puffed out. We started coughing. I got up on my knees and shined my light inside. There was a flight of steps, but nothing like the basement steps. There were five of them and they were cut right into the bare rock.

"Let's go," I said.

"In there?" said Roger.

"Oh, jeepo!" said T. J.

"It's a tunnel," I said. "It's got to be the way out. I bet it's how the runaway slaves made their way to freedom. Come on."

"Okay, Great Brain," said Roger. "After you."

I trained the light on the crude stone steps. Then I headed down. The bottom of the tunnel was dirt. The ceiling was pretty low, so we had to duck our heads. At least we didn't have to crawl, like adults would probably have to.

We inched along. Me first, then Roger, then T. J. holding the harpoon. There were no skeletons or bones, that we could see, anyway. I wondered if we were going south toward the water or north toward the road or east toward the woods around the property by the edge of the cornfield. My sense of direction was all mixed up.

Just then the floor began to slope up, and I could make out some crude stone steps just ahead. A way out! When we reached the steps, I shined the light up.

"Another trapdoor!" said Roger.

I pushed up hard on the door with my hands. It didn't move. There was no bolt or lock or anything to open.

"Help me push," I said.

Roger and T. J. squeezed themselves next to me. The three of us pushed up as hard as we could, T. J. pushing with the harpoon.

SKKREEEAKKK! The door slammed open.

We blinked to get used to the light, but it wasn't the bright sunlight I had expected. It was green and shadowy, almost as if we were underwater. It wasn't water, though. We were under a massive bush that had grown over and around the trapdoor. The leaves and branches were woven so close together over my head, I could barely move.

"Hurry up, Fish!" said Roger.

I scrambled to my knees and crawled away from the door.

"What the heck?!" Roger emerged.

"Ouch!" said T. J., lugging the harpoon.

Thorns and prickers and sharp vines jabbed at me. I could hear Roger and T. J. behind me. Finally, I pushed my way clear of the monster bush.

I stood up and took a deep breath. We were in a clearing, or what I figured was once a clearing. It was so overgrown, it was hard to tell. The grass was long and wild, and there were bushes growing all around. In the tangle of thorns and branches, a few of them still had some wilted blooms.

Yellow blooms. They were yellow rosebushes.

"The secret cemetery!"

We hacked our way through the tangle with our hands. All of us got pricked by thorns and branches. But we didn't care. We had to find the tombstone.

T. J. was the one who did. It was under one of the bushes with a few yellow roses still growing on it. The small gray stone had fallen over and was green with moss. We almost missed it under all the branches.

There was an angel carved on it, just like Great-Grandma O had said. We couldn't make out the whole inscription, but we could see the letters MAT A ROY and the date 1847 and then some words.

"What's that say?" said Roger.

I scrubbed off the moss and dirt with my T-shirt.

"Wif and moth," said T. J.

"Huh?" said Roger.

I squinted down at the letters. "Wife and mother!"

Roger and T. J. jumped and whooped. So Hannibal had married Matilda. She was real. And they had had a child. If they hadn't, her tombstone wouldn't have said wife and mother. Here was proof set in stone.

I stared at the old, long-forgotten stone. A flash of light suddenly hovered right over it. I blinked, but it was still there. I followed it with my eyes as it floated over our heads, up through the branches, and then it was gone.

The hairs on the back of my neck prickled. Was that . . . no, it couldn't be. I shook my head. All of T. J.'s ghost talk was getting to me. It was only a trick of the light.

It had to be, because there were no such things as ghosts . . . were there?

A WHALE OF AN ENDING

The phone rang just as we were getting in the car.

"I'll get it," said Feenie, scampering into the kitchen before anyone could stop her.

I slid into the backseat as my dad got behind the wheel.

"I wish they'd hurry," I said. "I don't want to be late."

"You mean you don't want to miss the chicken wings." My dad laughed as he looked in the rearview mirror to fix the collar of his volunteer firefighter shirt.

We were on our way to the Whooping Hollow Fire Department's 100th Anniversary Barbecue. A lot sure had happened in the past week. After we told the Captain about Matilda Royce's grave and the secret cemetery, he called the mayor and the town zoning board. Benedict Billings had bulldozers at the house ready to knock it down, but he couldn't. Boy, was he mad. There was a hearing at the courthouse. The Captain and Wallace went. Wallace's middle name did turn out to be Welcome, by the way.

Roger, T. J., and I weren't allowed inside the courtroom, but we got to wait outside. After all, we were the ones who found the cemetery and the whaling log and ship's diary. There was also what Ms. Valen discovered after she started digging through some old papers and books that Two O's mom found in Great-Grandma O's attic. One happened to be a copy of the birth records book. It turned out there was an entry missing in the library's copy for December 31, 1847, for Matilda St. Clair Royce, daughter of Matilda St. Clair Royce of Brittany, France, and Hannibal Welcome Royce of Whooping Hollow. BINGO!

Ms. Valen called a French librarian, who did some research about families in Bayonne. She found out that baby Matilda was sent to live with her grandparents in France, who changed her last name to St. Clair, like theirs. She thinks it was probably because Hannibal was away at sea too much of the time to raise a child alone.

It was pretty boring sitting out in the hall, until the Captain started yelling. "I tell you, this documentation is shipshape. The cat is out of the bag, Billings. Or, as we used to say in the Navy, your ship has sailed."

Mr. Billings started yelling, too. Something about trespassing and the rules of probate. Then the judge had to bang the gavel for a while. Roger, T. J., and I finally got called in to tell how we found the whaling log and the gravestone and stuff. There was actually an entry at the very end of the log dated December 1847 that read: *Have to get home to Matilda. The baby is sure to be born any day now. If only this leg would heal!* So, Matilda and their baby were the family he had to get home to, just like I had read in the *Whaling Masters* book. It was also how come Admiral Royce wanted the log kept safe and given to the right authorities, since it proved there was a whole 'nother branch of the Royce family.

My mom and Feenie got in the car.

"Who was on the phone?"

"Oh, some gardening company calling about—"

"Gophers," said Feenie, buckling herself into her car seat. "It was somebody called Mister Gopher Gone. I told him it was time to go to the barbecue."

"Oh, brother," I said.

There were lots of cars already parked at the firehouse when we got there. People were milling around with plates of food or sitting at the long picnic tables that had been set up in the back near the grills. The fire engines were parked out front, all shiny, even the oldest one from the first year the department opened in 1915. That didn't seem so long ago to me anymore, when I thought about Hannibal Royce.

"Dude!"

Roger and T. J. were heading my way, holding paper plates loaded with chicken wings.

"Wing?" said T. J.

I grabbed one and took a bite. Spicy barbecue sauce dripped down my chin.

"Whoa!" said Roger. "Check it out!"

"What?" I turned.

A long dark limousine pulled up. A man wearing a black suit and mirrored sunglasses got out.

T. J. dropped his paper plate. Chicken wings and barbecue sauce splattered all over us.

"What the heck?!" I said.

T. J. didn't seem to notice. His eyes were on the man in the black suit. "It's Dr. Ghost B. Gone. I can't believe he's here. . . ."

He wasn't the only one. Everyone was staring in surprise except Wallace. He was so pale, he looked as if he might hurl at any second. Maybe the chicken wings didn't agree with him.

"I'm here about the haunting," said Dr. Ghost B. Gone.

"He didn't just answer our call—he came," said T. J. "Wow!"

"How did he know where to find us?" said Roger.

All of a sudden, it hit me. Mister Gopher Gone was none other than Dr. Ghost B. Gone. "Feenie told him!"

Dr. Ghost B. Gone moved toward us with a smile on his face.

"Oh, jeepo!" said T. J. "Is he coming to talk to . . . to . . . us?"

"Well, we are the ghost hunters in this town," said Roger, puffing out his chest.

"He doesn't want to talk to—" I began.

"Wallace!" called Dr. Ghost B. Gone, moving past us to where Wallace stood with the Captain. "How are you? How's the house? What level haunting are we looking at here?"

"I'm not sure, sir," said Wallace. "I wasn't here on business—I mean, not Dr. Ghost B. Gone business. I was . . . that is . . ."

"You're looking at the great-great-great-grandson of Hannibal Royce, the famous whaler, who is now the owner of the old Royce house," boomed the Captain, wearing his Navy blue and gold, as he always did for a special occasion. He patted Wallace so hard on the back, his glasses fell off. "Tell everyone what you plan to do with the house, my boy," said the Captain.

"I want to fix it up and turn it into—"

"—a whaling museum of all the ridiculous things this town doesn't need," said Benedict Billings. "There's no money in museums. Condos and golf courses are what this town needs. That's progress." He held his card out to Dr. Ghost B. Gone. "I can help you find the perfect relaxation retreat after a hard day's work . . . um . . . ghost hunting."

"What about the ghost?" said Dr. Ghost B. Gone.

Roger, T. J., and I looked at one another.

"That ghost be gone," said Roger, and everyone started laughing, even Dr. Ghost B. Gone.

"Thanks to these boys," said Wallace, grinning at us.

"I'm pretty sure it was an orb," said T. J. all of a sudden. "At first we thought it might be an elemental, which is why we called you."

Dr. Ghost B. Gone smiled and handed T. J. his card. "Excellent paranormal investigating, boys!"

Everyone clapped except Bryce. He was straddling his yellow scooter next to Clementine.

Just then Mi and Si came running up to us holding a newspaper. "You're famous," said Si, reading the headline. "'A WHALE OF AN ENDING FOR AN OLD WHALER . . . Thanks to the sleuthing skills of three of our local boys—'"

"Wow!" said Two O. "You guys were really brave to go into that house and face the ghost and everything."

"Yeah," said Clementine, smiling at me.

"Big deal," said Bryce. "Since there was no ghost."

"Was so," said Roger, pulling his camera out of his pocket. "I'll sell you a peek for ten cents."

All week Roger had been selling peeks of the footage that was shot when he'd left his camera in the house. There were a few shadowy shots that might have been Wallace, and a few shots of what did look like a floating light. I kept saying it was just a trick of the moonlight or dust, but I couldn't help thinking about the light at the cemetery.

"It'll take a hundred kids for you to make a measly ten dollars," said Mi. "That's no get-rich-quick scheme."

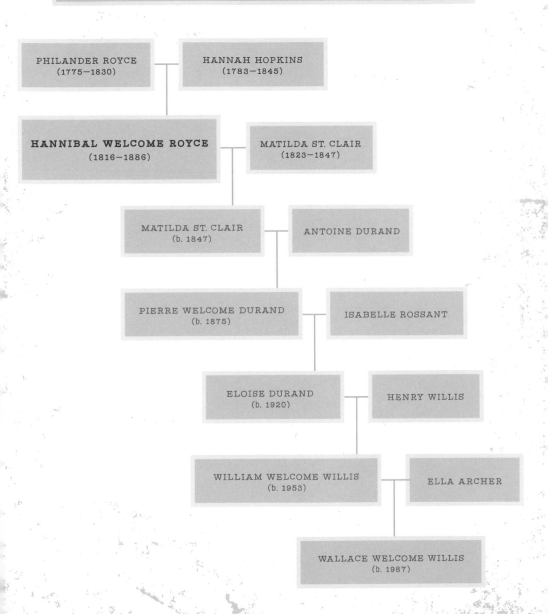

HANNIBAL WELCOME ROYCE — FAMILY TREE

•WALLACE WELCOME WILLIS BRANCH•

PHILANDER ROYCE
(1775—1830)

HANNAH HOPKINS
(1783—1845)

HANNIBAL WELCOME ROYCE
(1816—1886)

MATILDA ST. CLAIR
(1823—1847)

MATILDA ST. CLAIR
(b. 1847)

ANTOINE DURAND

PIERRE WELCOME DURAND
(b. 1875)

ISABELLE ROSSANT

ELOISE DURAND
(b. 1920)

HENRY WILLIS

WILLIAM WELCOME WILLIS
(b. 1953)

ELLA ARCHER

WALLACE WELCOME WILLIS
(b. 1987)

"I can do the math, Mi," said Roger. "This is just the beginning. I view it as advertising for the haunted house museum tour we'll be offering when the Whaling Museum opens. That will really rake in the bucks—or should I say clams?"

Bryce rolled his eyes at Trippy and True. "So, no ghost, and you never got the harpoon, either."

"We did find the harpoon," I said.

"In the basement near the secret tunnel," said T. J.

"You can read all about it in the newspaper, Billings," said Roger, pointing to the paper Mi was holding.

"You'll be able to see the harpoon as soon as the Whaling Museum opens," I said.

"You're still a loser," said Bryce, climbing on top of his cool scooter.

"Yeah, loser," echoed Trippy and True, who were standing beside him.

I opened my mouth to tell him to leave me alone when he revved his scooter engine with a *vroom*. All of a sudden it sputtered to a stop and the chain fell off. I watched as he wheeled it over to where Mr. Billings was deep in conversation with Dr. Ghost B. Gone.

"Um, Dad, can you . . . um . . . show me how to fix the chain, like you said you would yester—"

Mr. Billings shook his head with a frown. "Not now. Can't you see I'm working?" He waved Bryce away, and I heard him start telling Dr. Ghost B. Gone something about an ocean vista and a marble Jacuzzi tub.

Bryce just stood there with the saddest look on his face. The next thing I knew, my dad was standing next to him.

"The chain just needs to be centered so it doesn't pull to one side." My dad bent and pointed to the rear wheel. "All you have to do is align the rear wheel sprocket with the motor sprocket. I'll show you." He tugged gently on the chain. "There should be a quarter-inch play when the chain is properly tensioned. Here, you do it."

I watched as Bryce did what my father said. "Um . . . thanks . . . Mr. Finelli." He smiled.

"You're very welcome," said my dad, winking at Bryce. "You have a question, just ask. That's what I always tell my son."

Clementine met my gaze with an "I told you so" expression in her dark eyes. Now I knew what she meant. Bryce really was jealous. You would never know it, the way he talked about my dad. Feelings sure were complicated. It wasn't that they weren't real. They were just hard to see.

Kind of like ghosts, if you know what I mean. . . .

READ THE OTHER BOOKS IN THE FISH FINELLI SERIES!

PRAISE FOR THE FISH FINELLI SERIES

"A funny gem of a middle-grade mystery . . . a great boys'
counterpart to such stellar girls' series as Ivy + Bean."
—*Kirkus Reviews*

"This light adventure novel's winning humor shines bright,
brimming with nautical and pirate-themed wordplay
and wisecracks."
—*School Library Journal*

"Heavy on the yuks . . . Farber laces Fish's dialogue
with scientific and historic tidbits."
—*Publishers Weekly*

"A pleasurable read for the boy in all of us."
—*Library Media Connection*

"A feel-good chapter book perfect for reluctant
readers, particularly boys."
—Common Sense Media

"Go fish!" —*Kirkus Reviews*

"Plenty of action, humor, odd nicknames,
and nautical facts . . . a good choice for summer reading."
—*Booklist*